TIME FOR LOVE

HISTORICAL TIME TRAVEL ROMANCE-BOOK 2

NIKI MITCHELL

Time for Love

In 1890, Josie Goodwin believes in love and isn't about to marry for anything less—not even when her father demands she weds his business partner. After boarding a train to hide out at her brother's ranch, she never expects to land in the future—or to fall for the aggravating, alluring town sheriff.

Garrett Kellogg is not interested in love or a relationship.

He doesn't need a vivacious, time traveling woman in his bachelor life.

But Josie steals his heart—and then she vanishes.

❀ Created with Vellum

TIME TO SAVE A COWBOY is dedicated to my husband who always support my crazy ideas.

CHAPTER 1

Granite Heights, California
July 8, 1890

A SHARP RAP sounded on her bedroom door.

"Josephine Anne, your presence is required in the library," George Herbert Goodwin III, never suggested, he ordered.

"Of course, Father." Josie's stomach churned like cream becoming butter. The summons meant her father arranged for her hand in marriage to William Forsythe.

The dreaded union.

"I shall be there in a moment," her tone came out squeaky. She must contemplate a rational way to change Father's mind.

A dry wind fluttered the lacy curtains causing an icy chill to fill her soul. As a child, she would lie on her bed under the pink canopy and pretend to be a princess. Her prince in shining armor would show up on a white steed and rescue her. And they would live happily ever after.

But William was no prince, and she was no princess.

She longed for the type of love her mother's parents had shared, adoring how Gram and Gramps Smith's eyes shone as they gazed at each other. On occasion, she had seen the same look with her own parents, but it had seemed fleeting as the years went on. Father could be distant. Business came first and foremost in his mind.

If only her mother were still around.

Melancholy made her eyes misty.

Stop it. I must be strong when I speak with Father.

She did not hurry down the staircase. Her heels echoed in a slow staccato beat on the marble floor of the entry hall.

A dark paint square remained where the landscape she'd painted once hung—meaning father had sold off her favorite painting without even asking her permission. Vases, silver candlestick holders, and other household treasures vanished over the last four months. Money had become tight. She overheard her father talking with William about how he could save the day—in exchange for Josie.

Like a mallet hitting a railroad spike, her pulse pounded. She took a deep breath and entered the library.

"Josephine Anne." Father puffed his cigar from behind his massive mahogany desk. "I have joyous news. William has asked for your hand in marriage." He smiled, a smile she hadn't seen since she wore her hair in ringlets. "I have worried about your welfare. I am relieved to see a brighter future for us all."

A brighter future for her father. William owned the largest orange grove in Southern California. Four months ago, he talked her father in pouring his entire fortune into ventilated boxcars, promising him an account that would supply oranges across the nation. She had overheard their conversation the previous night. The orange deal would be sealed once the marriage occurred, making her the key to her father's success.

But a future with William would be impossible. The cad had cornered her at the Independence Ball last night. "Another month or two, and you shall be mine," he whispered before giving her a slobbery kiss. Even now, her stomach sickened.

Unable to remain silent, she blurted, "I do not l-love William and have no desire to m-marry him." Dash it all. She abhorred her stutter.

He let out a snort-like chuckle. "Josephine, dearest, you have been reading too many dime novel romances. True love develops over time. Once this union is blessed with children, you will grow to love your husband."

Never, she wanted to shout. Anger rose inside. Her fists tightened like an overwound watch. Father didn't care about heirs; he cared about having his debts disappear. In other words, he had traded her off like chattel.

"I have allowed you plenty of freedom while assuming you would choose a suitable husband well before now." In a little over a month, she would be twenty-two. A woman on the shelf. Considered spinster age.

Not that she minded the label.

"It's time you marry. William will make an excellent provider." With finality in his voice, he folded his arms, mimicking the portrait of her great-great-grandfather Goodwin hanging on the wall behind him—dour and unyielding. When father showed this temperament, she knew any retort on her part would put him on the defensive.

What she needed right now was time. "Father," she paused to think. "In order to create a perfect gown, my dressmaker will require at least four months." That wasn't exactly a lie. Even a simple day dress took a month or more to complete.

"Your mother would want you to wear her gown." Her father leaned forward, again smiling, but no humor mirrored in his eyes.

If she tried to argue this point, it would sound like she hadn't loved her mother. The truth was she missed her every day.

"William is making arrangements with the reverend as we speak. Six weeks will give you ample time to have your seamstress complete the alterations."

"Of course." She forced a smile, while inside she shuddered. Father assumed wealth created happiness—while at heart, she preferred a simpler lifestyle. She'd gladly trade expensive dresses and lavish parties to go back to the carefree summer days spent on the Silver Spur Ranch with her mother, brother, and grandparents.

"I am fortunate to have such a dutiful daughter." He picked up his cigar, flicked the ashes in a cylinder-shape ashtray and excused her.

No hugs. No affection. No consideration.

His attendant, Claymore, left the door open a few inches as he went into the library. “Sir, I have everything prepared for your trip to San Diego. Your carriage will be waiting within the hour.”

Yes! Father would be leaving.

She tiptoed to the stairway and ran up the steps.

CHAPTER 2

Present-day, Hesperia California

If only Garrett hadn't agreed to playact as the sheriff for the Founder's Day Celebration, especially after getting home from his emergency dispatcher shift at three. But the fundraiser took in money for a good cause—the abused women's shelter. The donations had already been paid, plus jars would be located in various places to collect more money. His task for today was to fake arrest specific people as a show for the visitors of Old Town and lock them in the old jailhouse for an hour. He gulped down a cup of coffee, needing the caffeine jolt.

Moments later, he set his fake holster on the floorboard and slunk into the passenger seat of his friend and roommate's mustang.

"Rough night," Zack asked as he backed out of the driveway onto the street.

"Just long." It wasn't the career he'd planned, however being a 911 dispatcher was a good job, an important job because he helped save lives. It would be even better when he got off the swing shift, and his evenings were free to go out and have some fun. He glanced over at Zack. "What's up with the black derby hat?

"I decided to look like Bat Masterson."

"Who?"

"You know, the gunslinging and gambling friend of Wyatt Earp." Zack liked to take these gigs to the next level. This event gave Zack an excellent opportunity to dress up. He gave Garrett a lopsided grin. "Bat was quite a lady's man. I intend to live up to his legend."

"Thus the suit and weird mustache."

"Chicks love mustaches." Zack wiggled his brows.

"Whatever." Garrett's phone buzzed. He swiped the screen and read the mayor's text.

Josie will be on the 3 o'clock train. Short ginger in a long blue dress. She's a Theatre Arts major and is excellent at her craft.

"I'm arresting the mayor's daughter, Josie. You know her?"

"Nope. Hope she's hot and likes to party. If not,

I'm sure we'll find a couple of cute girls at the club." Zack parked the car on the backside of the old town.

"Guess we'll have to wait and see." Garrett got out of the car and buckled his holster. Together they walked behind the blacksmith's shop on First Avenue. The anvil clanged.

Several yards further, Garrett spotted a high school friend securing a harness to a carriage. "Hey," Garrett called. "See you're giving rides again this year."

"Yep. Don't mind. Not when the money I raise goes to a good cause." He tipped his beige Stetson.

"Which is why I'm here." For the past three years Garrett had been roped into being sheriff. "We'd better go check in."

"See you around." Their friend waved them off.

Garrett and Zack crossed the street, went up a couple of steps to the boardwalk, past Carol's Confections, and strode inside the assayer's office.

"Glad you made it," Zack's Uncle Will said.

Garrett shook his hand. "Thanks."

Will opened the top drawer of an old desk and passed Garrett a silver star. "Here you go."

He pinned it to his leather vest.

"Catch." Will threw Zack a star with the word deputy engraved on the front. "Now you two look official."

Four women in long dresses came in. One lady spun her parasol over her shoulder.

"See you later, Uncle," Zack called while Garrett grabbed a jar labeled Donations for Abused Women Shelter, and they left the building.

Luckily, the cup of joe had finally kicked in and Garrett was ready for his day.

A couple minutes later, they moved up three weathered stairs to the jailhouse. Zack unlocked the door, propped it open with a wooden wedge, and the two of them stepped inside. The musky scent gave the tourist town an old-fashioned feel similar to Old Town San Diego or Calico Ghost Town. The original cells were about the size of a refrigerator box.

"This place smells like dirty socks." The window had no glass, so Garrett pushed a board out and placed a stick to hold it open.

"Makes me glad I'm on patrol first." Zack tucked his shirt into his pants and strolled out.

Garrett checked the schedule on his phone. "Our first show is at ten. We're arresting Principal Fowler and his son. You get the son, Ben. I'll snag the principal inside the candy shop."

"Sounds sweet," Zack joked and strode out.

One of the wanted posters flapped from the slight breeze. The noise would annoy him all day if he didn't do something about it. He searched the desk, found tape in the bottom drawer and fixed the poster.

A teenage boy and his girlfriend walked inside the office holding hands. She tugged him closer to the poster Garrett had just taped down. "This guy's a wanted horse thief," the girl said.

The boy pointed to the poster. "Did he ever get caught?"

"Don't know." Garrett thought little about it.

"I'll look him up." The girl got out her phone and called into it. "Find Dusty Mann."

"What's it say?" Her boyfriend leaned in.

"No reception. Let's go outside and see." And the two left.

The clock tower chimed ten times. The uncle called from outside the office. *"Zack's caught the son of the Fowler Gang outside the candy store. He thinks the leader's inside."*

Right on schedule. Garrett took a deep breath, went outside, and got into character.

Ready for his first charity arrest Garrett threaded his way through the crowd. He rushed along the dirt road, up the planked walkway, and weaved his way through the scattered throngs of people here to celebrate Founder's Day. An attractive blonde waved, and he tipped his hat. *"Morning miss,"* he said with a slight drawl.

"Hello." She slowed her steps, and a young guy walked up and put his arm around her shoulders.

Another block and he reached Carol's Confection. *"I didn't do nothing,"* Ben Fowler snarled as he tried to get out of his handcuffs.

"Be careful. The old man's inside." Zack motioned toward the store.

"You'll never get him," the son said.

"Shut up and keep moving." Zach pushed Ben forward.

Garrett strolled inside the shop, recognizing the signature goatee of his high school principal which now showed flecks of gray. Jim Fowler sprinted out the door. Garrett chased him, catching him outside the bakery and pressing his fake pistol into his back. *"Hands up, Foulmouthed Fowler."*

"What'd he do?" someone shouted from the street.

"Robbed the First National Bank." Garrett clipped handcuffs around his wrists.

"I'm innocent, I tell you."

"That's what they all say." Garrett kicked the man forward with his boot. *"Clear the way, people. This criminal's joining his son in jail."* They stepped off the boardwalk, crossed the dirt road, and passed the Law Office of Smith and Jones.

"That was fun," Jim said quietly as they entered the jailhouse.

"A barrel of laughs." Garrett locked Jim Fowler in the cell with his son. "Okay, Ben, how much are we raising?"

"A thousand for the pair of us." Jim sat on a chair next to his son's cot.

"Great. The shelter can use it." One of Garrett's friends and her mother had fled to the Whiskeyville Shelter because of an abusive stepdad. As far as he was concerned, the place saved their lives. He'd stayed in touch with his friend who was now happily married with two kids. Garrett shook Ben's hand between the bars. "Bet those twins of yours are getting big."

"I'll say. I thought terrible twos were bad, but they just phased into terrorizing threes." Ben pulled out his phone and showed him a photo of the boys covered in mud.

"My grandsons are pretty feisty. Reminds me of someone I know." Jim slapped his son's shoulders. "What've you been up to, Garrett?"

"Not much. I'm a dispatcher and working lots of hours."

"Sorry baseball didn't work out for you," Ben said.

Garrett swallowed down the bitter taste in his mouth. He'd played on a minor league team as a catcher and might have made it to the majors if a player hadn't slid into his hand with his cleats, the momentum breaking countless bones along with dislocating his shoulder.

"Sometimes life's not fair."

It hadn't been. Garrett had tried his best to look at the positives. He could still use his left hand, but his grip had weakened. He tried to shake off the negative thoughts that never did him any good.

A couple came in matching orange T-shirts. The woman pointed to the cell. "Are those two prisoners part of the fundraiser?"

"They sure are. You're welcome to add a donation." Garrett motioned to a jar on his desk.

The woman fished through her purse and added in a twenty.

"Appreciate the support."

"How do I go about throwing my husband in jail next year?" The woman motioned to the man next to her.

Garrett handed her a flyer. "Go to the Whiskeyville website and click on Founder's Day."

"You wouldn't dare." He hugged her to him. "But for a good cause I'd play along." The couple strolled out the door.

An hour had passed, and Garret opened the jail doors. "You two are free to go." His old principal shook his hand. "See you next year."

Zack's uncle came in. "Either of you boys hungry? I'm heading to Bertha's stand for a grilled hot dog.

"Absolutely. Mustard, ketchup. Sprite if they have it." Garrett reached for his wallet.

"It's on me," Zack left with Will.

Since nobody was inside, Garrett let out a long sigh. With nothing else to do, he opened the desk drawer, pulled out an old deck of cards and played solitaire. Funny, he'd forgotten how relaxing this simple game could be.

Zack came back with a cute blonde wearing short shorts. "This is Eve. I thought I'd show her what a real deputy does." He set a bag along with a soda on Garrett's desk.

"He follows my lead," Garrett laughed and took a bite of his dog.

"That's not what Zack said." Eve batted her eyes. "He says he does all the work here."

Garrett shook his head. "And you believed him?"

"Sure. He's the one out patrolling the town." She wrapped her arm around Zack's waist clearly staking a claim. "Anyway, I'm meeting some friends later tonight at the Wagon Wheel Saloon. You guys should come."

"We'll be there, sweetie," Zack wore a goofy grin. "Save room at your table."

"See you around eight. I'll meet you at the door, Zack, Garrett." The woman's hips swayed. Ripe. Waiting to be taken.

Garrett snickered. At least Zack should score tonight.

CHAPTER 3

1890

Josie paced to the window and looked out. Claymore held open the carriage's door, and her father got in.

Trepidation bubbled up her throat. If she planned carefully, she could escape her looming nuptials.

But where could she go?

Her thumb rubbed the gemstone of her necklace. Years ago, her dear brother, Dusty had found the heirloom in the attic of the Silver Spur Ranch. This gift reminded her of those special summers. Memories of trailing after her brother. A brother who loved her unconditionally. A brother who would be furious when he heard about the marriage her father had arranged. A brother who would support her decision to leave—or at least, she assumed he would be on her side.

Dusty suffered his own share of bad luck. After their grandfather's death, the bank foreclosed on the property and seized the family ranch. As heartbroken as he must have been over the loss, Dusty persevered. He now worked as the foreman at the Los Flores Ranch. A little over three years ago, she stayed in his small cabin. She loved the simpler lifestyle and had enjoyed helping the cook in the ranch's main kitchen, something that her father would have frowned upon. In his opinion, true ladies created menus and had staff do the work.

Now was not the time to reminisce. She needed a strategy to slip away.

According to Dusty's last letter, he still managed the ranch. She had an open invitation to visit him.

She would take the train to Hesperia and rent a horse to travel to his place. He would help her figure out what to do next. The idea of living on a ranch thrilled her.

She had some money. After her mother disappeared, father appeased Josie by giving her a generous allowance when all she really wanted was his love.

She must quit dallying. Time was of the essence.

To keep from having an unwanted visitor, she twisted the lock on her door.

Now what?

Her usual morning routine had her sketching in the garden. Not about to make the longtime housekeeper suspicious, she emptied her carpetbag used for art supplies and placed a box of pastels, paintbrushes and jars of paint, and stuffed the items in the bottom drawer of her dresser.

Now for clothing.

In her closet, she fingered the bustle of her pink satin gown. Her hand glided over a hunter green dress. The expensive ball gowns felt cold and meaningless. She much preferred wearing riding attire. Placing her favorite cowboy boots in the bottom, she also opted to take three waist-shirts, two floral skirts, a pair of pantaloons, a riding skirt, and a pair of denim trousers. She folded the items and tucked them inside her bag.

Opening the bottom drawer of her armoire, her hands trembled counting out five ones and fifteen silver dollars. A ticket to Hesperia cost a couple dollars. She slipped the bills and five silver dollars inside her alligator-skin pocketbook.

In a recent dime novel, she read about a woman sewing money into her petticoats to keep it safe.

Hitching up her skirt, she undid a section of the hem and stitched the remaining coins inside.

Dressed in a powder-blue waist-shirt and a navy skirt, she found the matching wide-brimmed hat to obscure her face from the townsfolk.

She reached the backdoor of the house. Her stomach knotted like a tangled skein of yarn as she stepped outside.

"Beautiful day." Hilda startled Josie.

"Indeed." She flashed her brightest smile.

Hilda held a cluster of carnations and gave a pink one to Josie.

The fragrance a reminder of spending hours outside gardening with her mother. Josie wondered what would happen to this servant who always treated her with kindness. "I won't be requiring dinner tonight." Which was true in the vaguest sense.

"Very well, miss. Enjoy your day." Hilda nodded and headed into the house.

To calm her nerves, Josie sat at a bench in the flower garden, appreciating the vibrantly colored petals of purple, pink, red, yellow, blue, and orange. Her mother once expounded on the names of each plant, but she never paid close attention. At the time, she'd preferred chasing monarchs, yellowtails, and spotted skipper butterflies.

She heard the back door shut. Time to leave. She pushed down the panic creeping up her spine.

Her plan must work.

Unlatching the back gate, she slipped out to the dirt trail leading to town, strode to Ninth Street, past five similar box-like houses, and found Old Mrs. Snyder working in her flowerbed.

"Josephine, I haven't seen you in ages," Mrs. Snyder called. "How about coming into the parlor and sharing a cup of tea?"

"Maybe some other day. Have a lovely afternoon." Josie waved as she walked off. Another two blocks further, she came to Santa Fe Avenue and the train station—her passport to freedom. She allowed herself a long sigh.

Uh-oh. Reverend Thomas sat on a bench not far from the ticket booth. *Please don't see me.* She pulled down her hat and walked past him.

"Hello." The Reverend lowered his newspaper and glanced at her over his spectacles. His wife and two children sat next to him. No doubt, they could hinder her from getting on the train.

Drat, in order to not look suspicious, she must stop and chat.

"I hear congratulations are in order." He took her hand. "I'm honored to be officiating your ceremony."

"Thank you." She gave him a bright smile, hoping he couldn't read her inner angst.

"I am happy for you, dear." His wife joggled an infant on her lap. "I imagine you have plenty of preparations to get ready for the big event."

"Yes, it shan't be an easy feat to accomplish in a little over a month." If she had her way, this wedding would never occur.

"Where are you off to this day?"

Okay, stay calm. Think of a plausible location.

If she mentioned she was heading for Hesperia, there might be questions about why she was traveling two hours away from home without a chaperone. "Today, I'm meeting a friend in San-San Bernardino."

"We're heading for Colton. You must sit with us," the wife said. Her two-year-old daughter sat close, squeezing her rag doll. How adorable.

"Allow me to purchase my ticket, and I shall be right back." Josie got eye level with the toddler. "You'll have to tell me all about your dolly."

She went to the depot ticket booth not much larger than an outhouse. According to the depot's schedule, the northbound train should arrive any moment and would depart at two-thirty. In line, she rocked back and forth on her heels. The shrill whistle sounded as she stepped up to the window and spoke softly to the clerk wearing wire-rimmed glasses, “One-way to Hesperia.”

The train slowed. The departing passenger’s shoes clicked and clomped on the wooden planking.

“That'll be a dollar seventy-five.”

She paid and was handed a rectangle parchment pass.

"Hello, Josephine. Are you here to greet me?" a deep voice asked.

She turned, staring into the round ruddy face of Nathaniel Forsythe, William's younger brother.

Oh no! What should she do? Remain composed—act normal. “I am helping the reverend and his-his wife with their children.” She pointed to the train. “They are boarding as we speak. Pardon me, Nathaniel, I must hurry in order to catch up with them.”

“I’ll tell William I saw you.” He tipped his hat.

“Please do.” Her pulse sped faster than one of her toy tops.

CHAPTER 4

Josie rushed to the closest passenger car and hurried up the tall grated steps. The reverend's wife waved Josie over.

That was close. Sweat beaded on her forehead as she took a seat next to the little girl.

The porter shouted, "All aboard!"

The train lurched and wheels clacked from underneath her open window. Fresh air circulated allowing her to inhale the marvelous scent of freedom.

Then she glanced at the reverend reading his Bible. She had been deliberately dishonest to a man of the cloth. Sinners burned in hell, didn't they? In her case, she figured God would understand.

Maybe not.

She had disobeyed her father's wishes. Still, she

would never be happy with William. Didn't she deserve true love? She focused on the toddler. "What's your dolly's name?"

"Bawba."

The wife clutched her infant on her lap. "That's her way of saying, Barbara."

Josie patted the doll's yarn hair. "Barbara's a nice name. I had a doll named Folly. Is that not silly?"

The little girl nodded. "Sii-wee."

The wife hugged the toddler with her free hand. "I imagine she'll be saying, 'silly,' for our entire trip."

The family got off in Colton.

She blew out a long breath and moved to an empty window seat. She could do this.

The train chugged along. She gazed out the window. Miles and miles of citrus groves were broken up by an occasional farmhouse or barn or pasture.

"Next stop Saaaaan Bernardinoooooo," the porter called. He paused beside her seat. "Anything I can get you, miss?"

"No, sir." Josie beamed. The next stop would be Hesperia.

A portly man sat at the bench directly across from her. He set *a* newspaper down on the side.

"May I borrow that?" She asked, pointing to the paper.

"Help yourself."

High Desert Weekly Gazette

Horse Thief, Dusty Mann, Escaped Before His Independence Day Hanging

She rubbed her eyes. She must have read it wrong. This cannot be her brother.

Horse Thief, Dusty Mann.

Her heart rose to her throat and stuck. Dusty was honest and principled. It must be a mistake. He'd never resort to stealing.

She read the article looking for information. On June thirteenth, Dusty Mann fled the Los Flores Ranch with a thoroughbred filly, Bella Sheba. He was apprehended by the owner of the ranch, Westin McGraw, on the same day. Dusty was convicted on July second. Thaddeus Sinclair, Dusty's attorney, demanded a retrial. The judge denied the petition and set the hanging for July fourth. But somehow, Dusty escaped on a train heading north, making him a fugitive.

Dusty Mann is wanted DEAD or ALIVE.

DEAD!

Bile crept up her throat. She imagined her brother lying on the ground, riddled with bullet holes, blood pooling across his shirt.

Her pulse stopped and she struggled to gasp in air. Her dear brother had to be alive.

"Are you all right, miss?" the man across from her asked.

This couldn't be happening. Her brother almost hanged. He would hang if he were apprehended. Shivering, she felt cold and numb inside.

"Here, use this, miss." The man handed her a handkerchief.

She wiped tears from her face. What should she do now? She was on her way to Hesperia with only a little money, and now, no place to go.

Blessed saints.

She needed to think. Come up with another plan.

"Thank you, sir." She gave him back his hanky.

"Notice you was reading about Dusty Mann. Got

a few friends who think he's innocent. Glad to hear he didn't hang."

Hang.

Coldness rippled down her back.

"You know him?"

"He is my brother," she blurted out.

"No wonder you're so upset. Anything I can do to help?"

"I am afraid not, sir." Leaving the family estate had been a mistake. Then she imagined marrying William and decided she had made the right choice.

From the window she watched the train climb the Cajon Summit. In another ten minutes, she would arrive in Hesperia and speak to the sheriff and Dusty's lawyer.

They passed Summit Station's loading dock. She recalled the first summer she had visited her grandfather as a young child. Riding in front of him as he supervised his cowboys. Coercing cattle in stalls and up a plank into a steerage car. She adored her visits to the Silver Spur Ranch and had vowed to move there when she turned eighteen. But her grandfather died six months before her birthday. His death took a deep chunk out of her soul.

The train curved around to the mortuary. She would do everything in her power to keep her brother from ending up there. A tear dripped down her cheek, and she wiped it away with her fingertip. She loved Dusty. He couldn't die.

She turned her necklace's stone to the front and held it in her palm. It felt warm. Absentmindedly she rubbed her thumb along the garnet—back and forth. Back and forth. Back and forth.

The room spun with colors similar to the toy kaleidoscope her father gave her as a child. She tried to focus, but everything seemed blurry.

Land sakes. What was happening?

Pain pounded in her temples making her dizzy, and she closed her eyes.

Brakes squealed as the train jerked to a stop. She felt for the sides of the seat and managed to keep the momentum from throwing her forward. Then she looked around.

Something was amiss.

Was there an accident? Had the train derailed? If that were the case, she would have heard panic, screaming, the sound of metal grinding. Besides, none of those reasons would explain her dizziness.

The portly man that had been seated across the aisle had left. In his stead stood a young man wearing a dark green collarless shirt with the words Cal-Poly Bronco written in black across the front. His short knickers appeared to have dozens of pockets.

"What in tarnation?" She covered her mouth, wishing she had not spoken the words aloud, and blinked at least a hundred times.

The man in the odd outfit stared at her. "You're not gonna puke, are you?"

"Puke?" She didn't know what he meant. It was rude to ignore him, but she did anyway. Sucking in several deep breaths, she felt a lot better. She marveled at the high back seats in royal blue velvet. On the walls, wood panels had been painted light yellow. It seemed peculiar to have every window shut tight. The compartment should be stuffy. Instead, she chilled air filled the room.

A voice from above called, "Passengers departing from the Whiskeyville Station may now exit."

"Why didn't we stop in Hesperia?" she asked but found the oddly dressed man already halfway up the aisle.

Right in front of her, a teenage fellow held a square box to his ear and talked. "Hey, I'm here."

"Are you speaking to me?" she asked,

He kept talking without acknowledging her. "I'm starving. How 'bout Burger King?"

A king named Burger in the desert? If royalty visited this very location, the town must have become rather sophisticated in the few years since her previous visit.

"Last call for Whiskeyville. Next stop—Daggett," a voice called from up above again.

According to the schedule, Daggett would be an hour's ride further. She'd better disembark here and hire a buggy to take her the short distance to stay at the Hesperia Hotel or walk if necessary.

In front of her on the train, a scantily clad woman in a short dress well above her knees must be on route to a saloon. Scandalized. She would rather starve than earn a living in such a dreadful way.

As she stepped off the locomotive, she peered at its orange and black color. No steam billowed. For that matter, it lacked a smokestack.

My goodness, she'd been oblivious to the locomotive's details when she boarded earlier.

CHAPTER 5

A train whistle blasted three times. Three o'clock. The mayor's daughter would be their last arrest, and then they'd wrap-up for the day.

"Need backup?" Zack asked.

"I should be able to handle Josie." A local legend propelled the myth of a ghost train—one that could be heard but not seen. At the back of his mind, he hoped for a phantom locomotive. He shook off the negative vibes and got into character. This arrest added to the charity donations, so he hurried along the boardwalk to the depot, shouting, "*Out of my way, folks. Outlaw Josie is reportedly on the train.*"

As he weaved his way toward the depot, people crowded the boardwalk. Some bystanders leaned against the building across the street watching. Two women in hoopskirts stopped in front of him.

"Excuse me, Ladies." They scooted to the side, allowing him enough room to step to ground level.

A kid, no taller than his elbows, stood beside him. *"You gonna arrest some bad guy?"*

"Actually, she's a gal. Outlaw Josie's getting off that train." Garrett pulled his pistol from his holster and spun it like a pinwheel. *"From what I've heard, she gunned down a little boy for asking too many questions."*

The kid frowned as his eyes widened.

A friend from high school put his hand on his son's shoulders. *"You best listen to Sheriff Garrett Mitchell, son. He's the second-fastest gun in the West."*

"Who's the fastest?" the boy asked.

His friend kneeled eye level with his son. *"His sister, Birdie."*

Garrett chuckled.

The train's bell clanged as it pulled into the depot. Garrett waited and watched as a gray-haired couple got off, followed by a blonde woman holding the hand of a little girl with pigtails. A puff of steam hissed from the locomotive's side hitting him square on the bottom of his boot.

Not what he expected at least he didn't startle. Okay. So far, the day hadn't been bad, and he was looking forward to meeting the mayor's daughter. Sparring with the lady might turn out interesting.

A petite redhead carefully took the train car's

grated steps to the platform. Her blue blouse and long skirt matched the description in the text. This must be Josie.

Pushing back the brim of her straw hat, her eyes darted to the right and then to the left.

A toddler moved toward the train's wheels. Knowing the train could lurch forward, he reached for the kid and grabbed him into his arms.

A frantic woman rushed over and took her child. "Thank you. I put him down for a second, and he shot over here."

"No problem." He was supposed to handcuff Josie near the depot, but she had taken off. He looked around and spotted her picking up the edges of her skirt as she hurried up the boardwalk steps.

She glanced behind her in Garrett's direction and continued toward the cigar shop. Half a dozen men in pinstriped suits and derby hats congregated outside watching an older fellow at the bench whittling.

The lady pushed up her bag on her elbow but didn't slow. Her motions were a bit jerky and tense.

The owner called from the shop's doorway, *"You after somebody, sheriff?"*

"Outlaw Josie," he called, practically sprinting.

She scurried past the Shooting Gallery Grill. Ten yards ahead, he spotted her wide hat at a vendor's table. She fingered a turquoise necklace, frowned at the price tag and moved on. Pausing at the next booth lined with paperbacks, she picked up a book and cracked a smile as she looked at the cover. Her cheeks blushed. She dropped it and rushed off.

He went right to the book, grabbed a Harlequin Desire with a hot shirtless paramedic. "Romance?"

"A buck and the books yours." The local bookstore owner chuckled.

"Why not?" He pulled out a dollar, then tucked the book in his jean pocket and spotted the woman several yards away. "Gotta run."

Glancing over her shoulder, Josie bumped into an older gentleman and kept on walking.

He caught up to her outside the bakery. *"Josie."*

She stopped and turned facing him.

"You are under arrest." He reached for her right wrist, pulling her to turn forward, and clicked a handcuff on her.

She snatched her left arm from his hand and sent her left heal toward his private parts.

He dodged the attack, bent toward her ear and whispered, "It's just an act. Cut the theatrics." The mayor had warned him she'd put on a good show. He reached forward, grabbed her left hand behind her and clicked the other cuff in place.

"Why are you doing this?" She dropped her bag on

the ground as she tried to get out of his hold. Then she kicked him in the shin and tried to run.

"Ouch." Somehow, he managed to hold onto her hands. "You don't have to get violent."

A crowd gathered around them.

"Got yourself a feisty one, eh, sheriff," someone called.

"Let me go." She squirmed. *"You ... you brute."* She stomped on his boot. For a petite gal whose head reached the bottom of his chin, she had a lot of power.

"Cool it! It's just a game," he whispered.

"Unhand me, or you'll be sorry." Her stance became rigid.

"Can't you see she's scared? Let her go," a woman shouted.

Josie tried to clomp on his boot again, but he moved his foot to the side.

"She broke the law. Outlaw Josie's going to jail. Out of the way, folks."

Will came along and picked up her bag. "Want me to bring this to the jailhouse?"

"Be obliged." He thought he felt her hands shaking. "Don't worry. Everything's okay," he crooned.

"How can anything be tolerable when you are detaining me?" Her purse had slipped down to her wrist and hit his thigh as they walked. "*Sheriff. I have*

done nothing wrong," her voice came out as soft as silk.

Dozens of people lined the boardwalk. They passed Daisy's Dolls and Toys and crossed the street.

"*You gonna lock up that poor defenseless woman, sheriff?*" a man asked from the doorway of the law office.

"*I'm getting to it.*" He rested his hands on her shoulders. "*Ladies and gentlemen, I need you to clear the walkway.*"

"*What'd that woman do?*" somebody shouted.

He nudged her forward. "*Miss Josie robbed a train.*"

"*I would never commit such atrocities,*" she said in a meek tone and her shoulders stiffened. She was quite good at role-playing, reminding him of an animal caught in a snare. Afraid. Ready to give a good fight.

"*Heard she murdered the conductor,*" another person called.

Garrett shrugged. "*Wouldn't surprise me?*"

"*You captured the infamous Miss Josie.*" Zack met them outside. "Great job," he whispered. "You two have the audience eating out of your hand."

She gave Zack a strange look like she didn't understand. A flash of uncertainty flickered across her face and for a moment this didn't feel like acting. He gazed into her bewitching turquoise eyes. Holy shit. Fear registered in her like a lost puppy unsure of the people around her. Something wasn't quite right.

Or he was reading too much into the situation. After all, her dad said she'd put on a good show.

"Relax and I'll get those off." Garrett unlocked the cuffs and stared at her. With her long lashes, wide mouth, and an outfit that emphasized her tiny waist, she really was quite a beauty. "For appearance sake, you need to be in there." He nudged her into an empty cell and closed the door.

"Please don't do this."

"You know it's only for an hour," Garrett said.

"And then I will be released?"

"That's the plan. I thought your dad already explained everything."

"My f-father?" She reminded him of a cornered dog.

What was it about her that drew him in and made him want to wrap his arms around her and tell her everything would be all right? He shook off his nutty thoughts.

She's just playing a role.

CHAPTER 6

Garrett went back to his desk and shuffled cards. Several people walked inside, and a tall man blocked his view of Josie. The woman fascinated Garrett, so he stood to watch her. He shouldn't keep staring but somehow couldn't stop himself.

"I fail to comprehend why I am being detained in this jail cell. I have not committed any crime." She called out and several people inched closer to the cell.

"Don't pay Miss Josie any mind," Garrett shouted. *"After robbing a train and shooting the conductor, she's right where she belongs."*

"I'm innocent." Josie gripped her fingers around the bars. *"Could one of you nice folks please make the sheriff see reason?"*

"You're quite talented," the tall man said. "Have you starred in any movies or TV shows?"

"I fail to comprehend what you are implying."

"Bravo. I love the way you stay in character." The tall man clapped. He pulled out a ten and tossed it into the donation jar.

A woman next to the desk picked up the jar, read the label, and threw in a five as did several other people.

"Much obliged," Garrett said.

A pair of gangly teens went to the wall and checked out the posters.

"$100 reward for the arrest of the forger, Alexander Cohen of Milwaukee, Wisconsin," one of the teens said.

"What's a forger?" the other guy asked.

"Someone who makes counterfeit money." The first guy punched his friend in the shoulder. "Look at this one. $500 Reward for Horse Thief, Dusty Mann. Wanted Dead or Alive."

"Cool," the other teen said.

Garrett could have sworn he heard Josie gasp. Glancing her way, her face had become chalky white. Uncertain why his need to protect kicked in, he called to Zack, "Bring Josie a bottle of water."

"Sure thing." Zack grabbed a bottle from the counter, unlocked the cell, rushing inside where she sat on the edge of the cot. He unscrewed the cap and handed her the water.

She squeezed the container and liquid spilled out of the top. *"Oh, my goodness."* Lifting her chin, she took a long drink.

"Are those posters real?" The first gangly teen asked Garrett.

"Nope. They're duplicates. The horse thief is from the late 1800s in San Bernardino County." The Wild West era fascinated Garrett. Who didn't like guns, horses, and wild times?

"That's rad," one of the teens said as they left the building.

"You okay?" Zack had pulled up a chair near Josie's cot and was talking with her. Always the flirt, Garrett had no reason for this attention to bother him. Still, his hands fisted.

"I believe so.

"That was some good acting." Zack took her hand. "You and Garrett do well together."

"It was no act."

Garrett looked over at Josie. Sitting on the bed, her hands folded. Attractive with her curly auburn hair and beautiful eyes. Eyes the shade of a blue gemstone, he could get lost in their depths. Turning to Josie, he said. "I'll text your dad and thank him for his donation to the shelter." He quickly typed in a message.

"Donation?" She blinked several times and grasped her hands together tightly. "I don't understand. Did my father ask you to detain me?"

"Of course."

Her brow quirked up as if surprised while her bottom lip quivered. "Please, sheriff, do not send me back to my father." Her tone was high pitched and almost desperate. What an actress!

People had cleared out, except for one older man. "Lady, you're really good." He dropped a twenty in the jar and walked out.

Garrett's phoned beeped, and he swiped the text.

Josie just arrived at our house. Won't make it today.

His blood shot to his face. How could he have made such a big mistake? "Oh, shit. The mayor's daughter never came." No wonder this woman looked scared. And now he'd have to backpedal and explain. He showed Zack the phone.

"You arrested the wrong woman, fool." Zack motioned for Garrett to step out the door.

His stomach twisted. It now made sense why she hadn't waited for him outside of the train depot, but he still wondered why she sounded like she had followed their script.

"So what if you made a mistake. You seem to like

her. Think we should ask her to the bar tonight." Zack's voice got quieter.

"She's cute. Maybe."

"Go for it, bro."

What did he have to lose? He went in and opened her cell door. "It seems as if there has been a mix-up. I thought you were the mayor's daughter."

"Does that mean I'm free to go?" Her eyes remained wide as she got up, smoothed out her skirt and walked toward the door.

"It does."

Zack folded his arms and mouthed, *"Ask her."*

Garrett wanted to but couldn't quite do it. "Before you go, I'd like to know your name."

"My name is Josephine … Josie." She paused for several beats. "Smith."

"It's weird. You matched the description I was given. And you both share the same first name." Whatever had happened didn't quite make sense. He was stumped. "I am sorry."

"Missteps happen," Josie said and scurried out the door.

Zack scrunched up his face. "Dude, you should go after her."

"I'll try and find her after I drop this off." Garrett grabbed the donation jar.

“Pie eating contest outside the bakery,” Will called from the boardwalk. “Starts in ten minutes.”

“I’ll lock up and join my uncle.”

Garrett rushed out, hoping to see the pretty petite woman in blue.

CHAPTER 7

Josie stepped outside into the bright sunshine and sucked in a deep breath of freedom. Getting handcuffed and thrown into a jail cell had only added to her oh-so-dreadful day. Earlier, when Garrett mentioned contacting her father, her heart sped faster than a galloping horse. She couldn't go back to Granite Heights. Wouldn't go back. At least her arrest had been a mix-up because she resembled the mayor's daughter. Still, she didn't understand why anyone would willingly spend time in jail, but supposedly they did it to earn money for a good cause.

"Excuse me," a woman behind her said.

Josie stepped to the right and inches away from the jailhouse front. The woman shot past her in pantaloons with a camisole top that showed part of her midriff. She held hands with a gentleman in dungarees. His most unusual footwear made a flopping sound as he walked.

Plum strange.

She glanced at a grassy knoll. Two women had on dresses so short they showed most of their thighs. My goodness. No one seemed the least bit shocked by such a display. Other men and women wore denim trousers and brightly colored buttonless shirts.

Taking a steady breath, she pulled her shoulders back and crossed the street. The sweet scent drifting from the confection shop tempted her to go inside. Saltwater taffy filled a dozen barrels near the front. She spotted a container of strawberry near the entrance. Since taffy was one of her favorites, she scooped half a dozen pieces into a bag and went to the counter.

The young clerk put the bag on top of a scale. It stopped at 2.4 ounces. "That'll be eighty-nine cents."

"You must be joshing?" Six pieces of saltwater taffy shouldn't cost more than a nickel.

"I only work here." The clerk gave her a goofy grin.

"She handed him a silver dollar.

He held it close to his eye. "1888. That's old. Sure you want to use this coin? It could be valuable."

"It's fine." Hardly old. The coin was minted two years ago. Her hands shook as she took the change and dropped it into her purse. What in creation was going on with this town? Her intuition told her something was amiss. Her legs seemed to move on their own accord, propelling her through the door and onto the boardwalk.

In front of her, a young man put his arm around a girl and held up a small four-inch boxy rectangle. "Smile," the man said.

"Let me see." The girl looked at the object he held. "Nice. Post that to twitter.

"What were these folks talking about? Her fatigued brain struggled to understand. Feeling out of sorts, she strolled through town and ended up at a table lined with various items. She fingered a silky scarf. A salesgirl stood behind her. "That's one of my favorites. It's a real steal for eight dollars."

The finest embroidered silk scarves made in France cost five dollars. She found this material sorely lacking, left the booth, and continued into the general store along the open aisle. Shelves and cabinets were filled with candles, tins of tea, toys, and various knickknacks and sundries. A rack of clothing held dozens of shirts on hangers. Proceeding to a shelf at the side of the room, she picked up a jar of boysenberry jam. *$8.95. For jam?*

Outrageous. Nobody in their right mind would pay that much. Setting the jar back in place, she pushed her way through the door and outside.

This blasted day had her frazzled mind seeing things. That must be it. After a good night's rest, she'd figure out how to find Dusty, and her life would make sense once again. Then she envisioned her brother's wanted poster. *Mercy*. She'd have to figure things out on her own.

Pushing her way through people crowding the walkway, a horse neighed. The carriage driver sat in the front seat holding the horse's reigns.

She stared at the man. He could take her to the hotel. "How much does a ride to the Hesperia Hotel cost?"

He tilted his head. "I'm only looping through Old Town Whiskeyville."

She shook her head. "Where may I find another carriage?"

The man chuckled. "Lady, it's late. Call an uber or wait at the corner for the city bus."

"Dash it all," she huffed in irritation and walked off, completely baffled at what to do. At the corner, she surveyed the area. Tied between two polls, a banner read, Whiskeyville—Celebrating Over One-Hundred Years.

One-hundred Years. This was a fairly new township. Her chest squeezed hard as if cutting off the oxygen in her brain.

No. That couldn't be real. She read the sign again.

"Blessed saints." Nothing made sense. There has to be a rational explanation.

The sign must be someone's idea of a joke.

Except things were not adding up, and a part of her wondered why?

Think.

Trace my steps.

She got on the train in Granite Heights. The locomotive totally bypassed Hesperia. Her head spun with pinpoints of colors like a kaleidoscope. The locomotive came to a stop in Whiskeyville. Once she departed, this town seemed off. Different. Both old fashioned and newfangled.

Her head ached. Spots floated in front of her eyes. Her legs felt like rubber, and she needed to sit down and figure this out. Placing her hand on the back of a wooden bench, she eased down and set her bag next to her.

She wanted to go home.

It hit her hard. The prices. The unusual clothing. People using vernacular she'd never heard before.

She peeked at the sign again. Could one hundred years have gone by?

If that were true, everyone she knew would be

dead. Dusty long gone. Her father gone. Her friends gone. Deep inside her soul she shuddered. A tear rolled down her cheeks.

She lowered her head and covered her face with her hands. Maybe she was dreaming. She shook her head. Her dreams had never been so vivid. She didn't want to believe she'd landed in the future. Still, she knew in her heart the crazy notion must be correct.

"Josie," a deep voice called.

Her pulse ticked fast. Moving her hands from her face, she gazed up to see Garrett's earnest smile. A familiar face in a sea of strangers. Her only lifeline—a man she'd just met.

"Are you all right?" In his gaze she saw concern and compassion.

"No." She felt like he actually wanted to help her, and right now she needed a friend. Pressing her fingers together like a vise, she chewed worriedly on her bottom lip.

"What's the matter?" He placed his hand over hers. Soothing. His gentle touch made her want to believe everything would be okay.

Should she tell him her real concerns? After a desperate day of fear and worry, her resolve had drained. She needed assistance, and his tender green eyes made her want to trust him.

"It's okay, Josie. I'm a good listener. My sister and

her friends tell me more than any guy wants to know about the female psyche. Whatever you have to say can't be any weirder." He sat down next to her on the bench and looked directly into her eyes, reminding her of Dusty. He had the same sincere expression. Whenever she had visited her grandfather's ranch, her brother would take time to listen to her, answer her questions and make her feel important.

"Are you hungry? I'm gonna grab a burger at the Shooting Gallery Grill. Why don't you join me?" Garrett gave her an endearing lopsided grin. "My treat."

His gorgeous eyes captured hers, causing her heart to flutter like a butterfly's wings. Mercy, he was handsome.

"In that case, I accept." She gave him a wobbly smile.

CHAPTER 8

Garrett offered his hand and helped her rise. "I'll take that." He carried her carpetbag containing changes of clothing, toiletries, and her favorite silver hairbrush. She carried her purse in one hand and clutched his firm muscular arms, all the while focusing on people's clothing. While she might occasionally wear denim or overalls riding around her estate, she would never consider appearing in town in such apparel. Her father would be furious if she attempted such outrageous behavior. Negative gossip tended to get back to him. Long ago, she'd decided it was much easier when he paid no heed to her.

"Why aren't the women appropriately dressed?" she asked, curious at the strange garments she witnessed.

He slanted his brow. "It's Founders Day. Some people dress up like the nineteenth century, but most girls wear jeans or shorts to be comfortable. The high desert gets pretty hot in the summer."

Again, it hit her that she didn't belong in this era. Her chest tightened, and her insides twisted in knots.

"Don't know how long I'd last in all that material you've got on. Bet you can't wait to change." On their way to the restaurant, they passed a tarp-covered booth. A woman who appeared to be about Josie's age wore a metal piercing in her nose and four earrings on each lobe. Her sleeveless blouse showed off a large tattoo of a unicorn on her upper arm. She couldn't stop staring. Only men got tattoos in her time and a facial piercing was unheard of.

"You into unicorns?"

Into? She didn't quite get his meaning but nodded anyway. Nothing was right, but dang if she knew what to do about it.

"We're crossing here. The grill's three doors down."

"Hey, Garrett." A blonde woman waved at him.

"Hi." Garrett tipped his hat at the pretty woman.

Josie should not be feeling a tinge of jealousy for the woman but did nonetheless.

They kept walking past a few shops. A line

wrapped down the street with people. The closer they came down the sidewalk the more she gripped Garrett's arm, not wanting to admit she was scared.

"I should've known this place would be crowded. You mind waiting?" he asked.

"Not at all." She clung to him, feeling like if she let go of him, she'd lose all sense of security.

"I'm getting a cheeseburger, fries, and a coke. You want the same?"

"That would be lovely." In this situation, she might as well have faith in Garrett's judgment.

"A table just opened up." He pointed to one right in front of them and handed her the carpetbag. "Snatch it, and I'll get the food."

She pulled out a chair and placed her bag along with her purse on it and watched him as he stood in line. Confident, he chatted with a man in front of him. Every now and then, he'd wave to her or tip his hat. She liked how he looked in his Stetsons. Cowboys like her brother and grandfather held a special place in her heart.

"You're in for a treat," Garrett set a red tray in the center of the table. His grin widened as he handed her a large, round sandwich wrapped in paper. He held his burger with both hands and took a bite.

She copied him and found the large sandwich

somewhat unwieldy but managed to eat a little. "This is delicious."

"I agree." He pulled off a paper covering and pushed a thin clear tube into a cup and sipped. Brown liquid came up.

Copying Garrett's actions, a frigid sugary caramel flavor filled her mouth. "Oh my. This is refreshing."

"It does hit the spot. I love fries dipped in ketchup." He passed her a small container.

She dunked the "fry" as he called it into the sauce and took a bite. "Tasty."

"I know, right." His eyes lit with a passionate flair, causing her heart to flitter faster.

She concentrated on her food. After a while, she peeked over at him and asked, "Do you like being the sheriff?"

"It's a fun part to play." He wiped his mouth with his napkin.

Part? He must be an actor. "Are you employed in the theatre?"

"Not hardly," he chuckled. "My real job is a dispatcher?"

"It sounds impressive," she replied not wanting to seem dumb by asking yet another question.

"It's not really. Calls can be pretty intense. And

sometimes I have seconds to make a quick decision, a decision that could save someone's life." He finished his sandwich, crumpled the paper and tossed it into a nearby trash bin. "Enough about me. Where are you from?"

"Granite Heights." The words just spilled from her mouth before she thought about it. Should she tell him more?

"That's outside of Riverside, right?"

"Correct."

"Birdie, that's my sister, has a friend whose family bought a ranch in that area. It's pretty."

"I love riding in the hills during the spring when flowers are in full bloom." Besides painting in the garden, riding had been another favorite way to escape the confinement of the cold mansion. The thing she would miss most in Granite Heights would be her sweet quarter horse, Duchess.

"You ride horses or motorcycles?" He asked, his deep masculine voice breaking into her thoughts.

"Horses."

"We've got some good stock where I live. We should go out sometime. Maybe take a ride along the river."

"I would like that." She imagined Garrett atop of a black stallion racing next to her, making her wistful and somewhat giddy. She pictured them picnicking in the forest while he held her hand and said sweet nothings. Her cheeks heated—a sure sign she blushed. Then, she glanced at a banner, and the thrill vanished. "Has Whiskeyville really been a town for over a hundred years?"

Garrett squinted at her. "According to the sign it was founded in 1889. If you could go back in time would you want to live in the Old West?"

"Y-yes." She understood her old life better than this one.

"Not me. I think living back then would be pretty harsh."

"Harsh? What do you mean?"

"It'd be like camping. No running water, electricity, internet."

She wondered how much things had changed in the last century. Running water in every home sounded wonderful. From what she knew of electricity, it seemed dangerous. And into-net. Another unknown word. She squeezed her cup. It wasn't glass and felt like something in-between an oilcloth and a piece of paper but smoother. "What material is the cup made from?"

"Paper, I guess. Anyway, what are your plans for tonight?" He gave her an adorable lopsided grin.

"I need to hire a driver and secure a hotel room." She had eighteen dollars and hoped she could stay for several nights. "After the day I've had, I believe once my head hits the pillow, I'll be asleep."

"Zack drove here. I'm sure he wouldn't mind giving you a lift." Garrett slipped his phone from his pocket and tapped on it. A few seconds later it chirped. "Zack will meet us at his car in about fifteen minutes."

Even though she hardly knew Garrett and Zack, her intuition said they were honorable. Besides, who else around here would be willing to help her?

"Zack and I are going out dancing later tonight. We could pick you up at the hotel around eight if you're interested."

A part of her wouldn't mind an evening out, especially if it meant dancing in Garrett's arms.

"It'll be fun. I promise I won't step on your toes." He winked.

"It sounds intriguing, but—I am a bit weary."

"Let me have your phone, and I'll put in my number just in case you change your mind.

"I don't have a phone."

"No phone." He looked perplexed for a moment. "I'll write it down." He grabbed a napkin, scribbled something on it, and handed it to her. "Here you go."

She tucked the napkin inside her pocketbook.

He picked up the tray and threw the items into a rubbish container. “Ready?”

“I suppose.”

CHAPTER 9

"You sure went all out with your outfit today." Garrett held up Josie's carpetbag as they walked up the street.

"As did you." She forced a grin.

"Not really. Already had the hat. Found the vest at a thrift store."

"Oh." She assumed a thrift store carried less expensive clothing.

WOOSH sounded from above. Her heart thundered against her chest as she looked up. A gigantic silver bird floated across the sky. "What is that monstrosity?"

"Just an airplane."

"Airplane?" She eyed the metal object in the sky. What the devil was an airplane?

"Are you all right?"

Her heart nearly shot out of its chest. She paused to collect her thoughts. "It's been a long day. I got on the train in 1890 and …" She almost covered her mouth.

"I get it. Riding on trains makes you feel like you've gone back in time."

Except when she boarded the locomotive it *had* been the nineteenth century.

They passed the visitor center, and she slowed at a rack with booklets about Whiskeyville. "Mind if I take one."

Garrett reached over and plucked a pamphlet from the rack. "Here you go."

She flipped open the page about *Whiskeyville History.* She read as they walked along. "Did you know that the depot was originally built in 1888 by local cowboys?" she asked.

"I thought it was 1889."

"It says here the building was erected in 1888 by the railroad as a place for workers to rest while changing shifts."

"Interesting," he laughed. "What else?"

"The front entrance of the General Store built in 1889 burned in 1974." Reading the year 1974, she sucked in a deep breath and continued. "The historical society restored it to the original blueprint."

"I'd never guess. Whoever worked on it did a good job."

Strolling to the corner, she glanced into the window for Dottie's Dolls and Toys. "Do we have time to look at this display?"

"We've got a couple minutes."

"I'll be quick." She inched towards the porcelain dolls in the exhibit. They looked like the ones she had lining her shelves at home. One had ringlets of red hair. She stepped closer and bumped into an older woman. "Pardon me."

"No problem. I just love these antique dolls." The older woman pointed to one with a hunter green dress. The fabric appeared discolored. Old. Worn. "My great-great-grandmother had one like that. We donated it to a museum."

Great-great-grandmother? Josie must be as old as that person—which was beyond belief.

"It was nice talking with you, but I'd better get going." The woman scurried off in her blue jean pants and a sleeveless top.

"Do you collect dolls?" Garrett asked as he moved behind her.

"Don't all girls?"

"Not my sister. She prefers stuffed animals." The twinkle in his eye gave her the impression the two must be close.

They curved behind several buildings to a walkway made of smooth white cobblestone.

"Hey," Zack trotted up next to her. "You guys should've gone to the contest. One guy downed fifteen pies."

"Was that you?" Garrett asked.

"Not this time." Zack turned to her. "You going out with us tonight?"

"I tried to talk her into it, but—" Garrett tugged her closer.

"It'll be a blast," Zack said.

"I'm tired and need to check into the Hesperia Hotel."

The corners of Garrett's mouth quirked downward for a second. Was that because she declined his invitation to go out?

"That's not far. We can drop you off and pick you up later," Zack said.

"Maybe." Creosote bushes and Joshua trees lined the uneven path, and she moved toward the middle of the road

Beep! A horn blared.

"Watch out!" Garrett grabbed her arm and pulled her to the side. He turned her to face him. "That car almost hit you."

"A c-car." Her hands became clammy, her legs trembled, and she wanted to run as fast as she could away from this crazy world.

"Are you alright?" Garrett said sharply.

Far from it, but she didn't want to admit the real truth—she was scared. "I don't like loud noises."

"Okay," he said, and they were walking again.

Zack gave her a friendly, country-boy grin. "Getting thrown into jail when you didn't expect it must've surprised you."

"It did." She nodded. Her unease was caused by way more than being thrown in a cell.

"The mustang on the end's mine," Zack announced.

She jumped at a chirping sound.

Garrett pulled on a handle. The door opened. "I'll sit in the back." He pushed the seat forward and climbed in.

Zack set the seat upright.

She stared at the padded chairs, low to the ground. She still wasn't too sure about her situation, however, getting into Zack's car seemed to be her safest choice. Bending her knees to move inside, her corset pinched.

Zack shut her door, hopped in on the other side, pulled on a strap and clicked it in place. "Buckle up."

She copied his actions. The strap tethered her against her whalebone corset causing it to dig into her ribs. Mercy, it smarted.

The surface in front of Zack displayed squares and circles and knobs. Intriguing. He pushed a button and a hum vibrated beneath her startling her. Pulling on a stick, he held a wheel with his left hand, looked behind him, and the car moved backward.

At the sudden motion, she gasped and gripped the sides of her seat, holding on for dear life.

"Relax, Josie. I'm a good driver." Zack moved the stick, and the car jerked forward onto a black surface and sped like a bullet being propelled from a gun.

"Mind if I turn on the air?"

Unsure what he meant, she nodded. A blast of cold air hit her face from the side. She placed her hand up to a hole in the dash. A steady stream of cold air blew out, chilling her fingers. "This is refreshing."

"Just got the air fixed." He twisted the knob a notch. "If you get too cold, close one of the vents."

She glanced out the window and watched the car speed along unfamiliar territory. She couldn't remember ever moving so swiftly and smoothly. The vehicle lacked any rocking action when compared to riding on a train.

Music blared, and she had to admit she enjoyed the fast beat. How was the sound possible without the assistance of a band or at least a graphophone?

"What brought you to Whiskeyville?" Zack asked.

She coughed and tried to get her bearings. "I thought I'd find my brother."

"Why didn't he meet you at the depot?"

"He was unaware of my visit."

Zack quirked a brow.

"I originally planned to get off at the Hesperia Station, but … well … I somehow missed the stop."

"There's no stop in Hesperia." Garrett said from behind her. "Do you have his number?

"I do not."

Zack gave her a sideways glance, pulled onto a long driveway, up to a three-story building, and slowed underneath a covered entrance with HOTEL lit in bright red letters. NO VACANCY flashed through the glass door. How could the sign have light inside?

"Looks like there aren't any rooms, Josie. What do you want to do?" Garrett asked.

"Is there another hotel nearby?" She choked out the words hoping to calm her trembling nerves.

"Check your phone. See if you can find any vacancies in Surprise Valley." Zack turned to Garrett.

"Siri, check for an available room at the Surprise Valley Hotel for today," Garrett said.

"Would you like me to connect to the website?" a woman's voice sounded.

How did someone named Siri get into the car? Josie turned and looked into the backseat for the person. Only Garrett sat there.

"Yes, please connect." A few seconds later Garrett grumbled, "There's nothing. I forgot how the hotels around this area fill up for Founder's Day."

"Want to call and have someone come and pick you up?" Zack asked.

"I have nowhere else to go," she muttered. Her hands trembled, and she clenched them into fists.

"What about the brother you mentioned earlier?"

"I haven't seen him in a couple of years. I came here hoping to find him. The last I knew he worked at Los Flores Ranch."

Zack's lips thinned, and he gave her a strange look. "The property sold a while ago. I know someone who used to work there. I'll ask around." He placed a hand over hers to comfort her. "We have an extra room. You can stay with us tonight."

"Good idea. We'll try to figure things out in the morning," Garrett agreed.

"We live in a converted bunkhouse. My cousin, Kristy, rooms with us. She's cool. I think you'll like her," Zack said.

She released the breath she held, grateful there would be another woman in the house.

"What do you say?" Zack glanced over at her.

"Yes." It wasn't as though she had any other options.

"Now that's settled. Garrett, you'd better call first and give Kris a heads up."

"Hey Kris, thought I'd warn you we're having company."

"Put her on speaker," Zack said.

"Say hi to Josie. She's staying with us tonight." Garrett held the voice box between the front seats.

"Hi, Josie," a woman's voice floated in the air.

"Hello. I hope this isn't a huge inconvenience." Josie tried to keep her voice steady.

"Of course not. It'll be nice to have another female around." Kristy sounded pleasant. "Just so you know, the guest room is kind of a mess."

"I'm thankful to have a place to sleep." Josie would have a roof over her head tonight. She had escaped an arranged marriage and somehow ended up in this mysterious future world.

CHAPTER 10

Garrett held the door for Josie. One little smile from her and his body stirred. Crazy. He followed her into the house.

"Hi." Kristy took the headphones off and looked up from the couch. The perky blonde flipped her ponytail to the front. "Love the outfit."

"Thank you." Josie smoothed out her long skirt with her hands.

"Have a seat." Kristy motioned to the couch, and Josie eased into it. "Want a beer, soda, maybe a glass of wine?"

"Wine would be splendid."

"I'll get it," Zack said.

"Grab me a beer." Garrett sat in the closest chair to Josie, all the while unable to take his eyes off her. He found her sexy as hell.

"You're going out with us, right?" Zack handed her a glass and took his usual chair facing the TV.

Josie sipped her wine. Garrett wanted her to come out with them tonight and get to know her. Tomorrow he'd do what he could to help her locate her brother, but until then he'd sidle up close to her and see where the night might lead.

"You've gotta go." Kristy crossed her legs and jiggled her foot. "You can line dance or play pool or just hang out. It'll be fun."

"In that case, how can I refuse?" Josie's lips quirked up, and he focused on her full, sensuous mouth. Damn, she was pretty.

"Let's get you settled in your room before getting ready," Kristy stood.

Josie downed the rest of her wine and got up.

"You need help with your bag?" Garrett offered not quite ready to let her go.

"No thank you." Josie got up. Clutching her bag and purse in her right hand, she followed Kristy to the stairs in the back of the house. "I hope my stay is not too much of an imposition."

"Any friend of Zack and Garrett's is welcome. I just put clean sheets on the bed last week," Kristy said as they turned the corner.

"You're into her," Zack's voice startled him.

"She's different." Even though she was a complete

contradiction to the women he usually liked, Josie drew him like a horse to alfalfa. Petite, not tall and leggy. Hair auburn red, not blonde. Reserved, when he tended to go for outgoing. But those expressive blue eyes reeled him in.

WAGON WHEEL SALOON

Two hours later, Josie hesitantly stepped into the very first saloon she'd ever been inside feeling decadent and somewhat wayward. Respectable women wouldn't dare set foot in such an establishment, except Kristy didn't act like a soiled dove. It dawned on Josie that she was a fish out of water in this new century. The idea that she had somehow traveled through time had her baffled. Still, she lifted her chin and marched ahead determined to make the best of her new situation.

At least she looked the part of a modern woman. Kristy had loaned her a stretchy capped-sleeved blouse insisting the turquoise color matched her eyes. Since Kristy had on what she called "jeans," Josie opted for the same. Thank goodness her new friend let her borrow a pair that fit way better than the stiff denim trousers she had packed. She liked wearing trousers while riding astride on her father's estate, giving her a sense of freedom.

It took a few seconds for her eyes to adjust to the dimly lit room. Loud twangy music played.

"You made it," a woman greeted them at the door and quickly dragged Zack past a long bar and toward a dance floor near the back of the room.

"Why don't you two snag a table, and I'll get drinks. You want white or red wine, Josie?" Garrett asked.

"White." There must have been dozens of tables to their left, all of them filled except for three or four by the wall. The lack of tablecloths gave the place a rustic feel. She glanced through an open doorway and spotted several men playing billiards. The game looked interesting.

Once in her seat, Kristy turned to her. "I love this place. It's loud and quaint. Give me a couple of drinks, and I'll be ready to dance all night. You line dance?"

"I've never tried."

"It's easy. Just follow me, and you'll get the steps in no time." Kristy grin made her feel at ease.

"Here you go?" Garrett's enchanting deep voice caused a shiver of heat to run up and down her spine.

She sipped her wine and watched the far-right

corner where eight to ten couples swayed and glided on a wooden floor.

"Let's dance." He reached for her hand. The simple touch made her warm all over. "*The Git Up's* a great song to two-step."

The music had a fast beat, and she wasn't sure she could pick up the steps. "I do not know this dance."

"Doncha worry. I'll lead. Just think quick, quick, slow, when we move." He yanked her to him, placing his hand near her shoulder blade and grasping her right hand in his.

Her fingers lay on his muscular biceps. A slow ember spread through her body. Held tight it was as if she were floating across the floor. Then she stepped on his toe. "Sorry."

"No problem. You're doing well." He gave her a disarming smile, and dang if her mind turned to mush. "You wanna try a turn?"

"Why not?"

He turned her under his arm, the momentum causing her to bump into another couple.

He laughed, really laughed.

A hum bubbled up her throat, and she found herself laughing too. Then the song ended. "That was fun."

"It sure was," his deep voice excited her from inside out. My goodness, this man oozed charisma.

A slower tune played. This time he held her even closer. She nuzzled into him and got lost in his spicy, masculine scent. Her father would turn over in his grave if he saw her acting like this. The heck with him. Her hand roamed up Garrett's arm and lay across his chest until the song ended.

"Ready to Wobble?" Kristy stepped next to her.

"W-what is that?"

"It's really easy. Listen to the words and follow me." Kristy jumped forward.

Josie moved forward, but everyone had jumped back.

"Okay, twist and wobble to the right."

Josie watched Kristy and couldn't help laughing as she tried to do the silly move with her hips. She eyed Garrett.

He gave her a goofy grin and did a quarter turn. My gosh, his grin made her heart flutter. "Come on, Josie. Show me your wobble."

She knew wiggling her hips as she did might be provocative and a little bit naughty, but she didn't care. Everyone else was dancing the same. By the time the song ended, she was breathless, her face flushed, and she couldn't help smiling.

Garrett slid his fingers into hers. "Pool table's open. You up for a game?"

"Absolutely." One of her father's friends had a billiard table. Only men were allowed to play. In this era women obviously were not excluded.

"What do you say?" Zack put his arm around the same woman who met him at the door.

"I'm parched. Let's go get a drink."

"Kristy's still dancing. Looks like it's just us two. You ever play?" He squinted at her.

"Never, but I am more than ready to learn."

"Then we'd better hurry before someone else steals the table." He held her hand as he led her into the other room, arranged the balls inside a plastic triangle and raised it off. "Grab a stick off the wall."

She picked the lowest stick. "This okay?"

"Yep." He took his own stick. "Hold the base with your right hand, rest the narrow end on top of your left. The object is to have the white ball hit another ball into one of the pockets."

"It doesn't seem hard."

His closeness made her body quiver.

"It's pretty easy."

He wacked the white ball. It scattered the rest of the balls, and three dropped in the holes. "If your first ball is solid, you'll be hitting in all the solids.

Your competitor has the stripes. Don't sink the eight ball. It goes in last. Grab a cue. I'll help you."

She put the end of the stick behind the cue ball.

"Focus on the ball." Mercy, his hands were over hers while his breath tickled her neck. "Use just a touch of pressure and aim for the corner."

She pushed her cue. The balls spread out with one striped ball spiraling into the corner pocket.

"Looks like you're stripes." He backed away, his big hands left hers, and she longed to bring them back. "Keep your head down when you take your shot. Aim for the ball closest to the center-left pocket."

She hit the white ball. It tapped the striped eleven and stopped near the edge. "Land sakes. It should have gone in."

Garrett walked toward the ball and blew on it, causing her number eleven to slip into the pocket.

"Isn't that cheating?" She fanned her face.

"Not at all. It's my duty to help a damsel in distress." His sultry voice made her all gushy inside.

"You're real Prince Charming," she teased.

"More like a Dudley Do-Right."

"Who?"

"A Canadian Mountie who saves his girl from peril." He edged to her side.

Did he consider her his girl? What a ridiculous

notion, a notion she really wanted to hold on to for some odd reason. "He sounds like a wonderful man."

He gazed at her, and my oh my, her face heated. "He's a character from a movie." His brow rose.

"Oh." She wanted to ask what in tarnation is a movie, but that might tip him off that she didn't belong in this century. "Well, this time I am going to hit that ball into the hole. Do you have any suggestions?"

"Find your shot and line up the best angle with your cue." His focus remained glued on her as he stepped to the side.

She walked around the table, looking for her best shot to knock that silly ball into the pocket. She lowered her chin, focused on her goal, set her elbow back and made contact with the striped fourteen which rolled into the pocket.

"You did it." He pulled her into his arms. "Let's see if you can repeat that." His eyes shimmered with mischief.

"You bet. "Distracted by him as she hit the ball, it skipped off the table and banged the shin of a person with a long ponytail playing darts.

"Ow!" A bearded man glared her way. "Who did that?"

Uh-oh! A crazy impulse made her point to Garrett.

He shrugged and said, “Sorry.”

The man shook his head.

As she pushed a wayward strand of hair behind her ear, a laugh slipped out.

“You’re a little sneak.” Standing behind her, he placed his hand on her shoulder and pressed his lips against her cheek.

And blessed saints, she wanted his mouth against her lips.

“Guess we’ve done enough damage here. Let’s head to our table.” Taking her hand, he led her into the other room where Zack, Kristy, and a few others sat.

The waitress approached their table. “Last call. What’ll it be?”

“Beer for me,” Garrett said. “White wine for Josie.”

CHAPTER 11

An hour later, Josie walked into the house feeling over the moon after a marvelous evening in a saloon—no less. She'd drunk several glasses of wine and played pool, but that wasn't what kept a perpetual grin on her face.

Garrett held her close while dancing. His full lips twitched upward into a smile. Each time his hand held hers, a pleasant tingle shivered through the center of her body. A couple of times he leaned so close she thought he might try to kiss her, which she wanted even though she knew it was improper. Nice young ladies didn't kiss men they just met.

"Come on." Kristy snatched her arm. "Let's chat while we get ready for bed."

Josie got halfway up the stairs. Her eyes met

Garrett's, and she couldn't resist adding a little sway in her walk.

"Since you forgot to bring your makeup, I'm assuming you didn't bring any remover."

Josie nodded. Kristy had assisted her in applying eye shadow, mascara and lip rouge.

"Then you can borrow mine."

"Thank you." She followed Kristy into her room which had an adjoining bathroom. Kristy offered her a moistened cloth. Copying Kristy, she wiped off her eyes, washed her face with a creamy soap and added a cold cream.

"Aren't you glad you went out with us?"

"Yes. I had a delightful time."

"You sure seemed to. I saw the way you looked at Garrett. You like him, don't you?"

"He is charming." Her cheeks heated as she recalled being held in his arms as they danced.

"Charming, you're funny." Kristy giggled. "But he's a good guy. His grandparents own the adjacent property to ours. I've known him most of my life so he's like a brother to me."

"Brother?" Pain gripped her heart, squeezing it like a tourniquet. Her own brother was a wanted man.

"Yep. Annoying and exasperating one minute. Protective the next."

"It's nice you two are close." Given Dusty remained in another century, she'd never see him again. And if he hanged? She sucked in a deep breath.

"What about your brother?"

"I rarely saw my him. My step-brother never got along with my father."

"That must've been rough."

"It was. On the positive side, my best friend, Elizabeth, lived in a home kitty-corner to mine. Last year she married and moved across town, so I didn't see her much after that." She and Elizabeth adored racing through the meadows near their home, galloping faster than the wind.

"That's how I feel about Garrett's sister. We're still besties, but life keeps both of us busy."

"Does she live next door?"

"I wish. She lives in Colorado but is here on vacation." Kristy had a faraway look. "She's staying at the beach for a few days, but we're planning mani-pedi's next week."

"What's that?" She brought her hand over her mouth.

"Manicures and pedicures." Kristy held up her hand, showing off blue nails with tiny palm trees. "I've been on a tropical kick lately."

"They're pretty. Did someone paint each tree?"

Josie looked at her plain nails. Clean, they still shone with the Rosaline enamel she'd coated on them two days ago.

"They're decals."

Unsure what that might be, Josie decided she'd ask another time.

"Did you see the guy with the black Stetson I danced with? His name is Clint." She stripped off her blouse.

Josie looked away. "He's very handsome. Are you two courting?"

"Courting?" Kristy gave her an odd look. "That's an interesting term. I like it." she put on a long shirt that reached her knees. "Although, I wouldn't mind dating him."

"Why don't you?"

"Good question. I guess I could ask him out for coffee or something, but I just can't. I'm kinda old-fashioned that way. I think the guy should make the first move."

"And he has not offered his calling card."

"You into Jane Austen?"

Josie had consumed every novel, reading each one countless times. The author had been popular in her day, and obviously her works still prevailed in this century. "What girl doesn't enjoy Pride and Prejudice?"

"I prefer Emma." She gave a wistful sigh. "I wonder what it would be like to have a man declare his undying love."

"As long as it's the right guy." She yawned. "I believe the late evening has caught up with me. Thanks again for loaning me the blouse."

"Keep it. The color washes me out."

A happy giggle escaped. "You are sweet."

"That's me, gumdrops and lollipops." Kristy gave her a silly grin. "You still leaving tomorrow?"

"That's the plan." At least it was, but with the prices she'd viewed, she had no idea where she could afford to stay.

"Too bad. I think we could become good friends." Kristy reached out and hugged her.

"So do I." This wonderful, accepting stranger had taken Josie under her wing, seeming to like her for herself not for her social standings or her family's prestige.

"Give me a call next time you're in town, and we'll go to the mall and grab some lunch." Kristy scribbled some numbers on a pad of paper. "Don't leave without saying goodbye."

"I won't." If only she could stay here a few more days.

CHAPTER 12

Josie woke on a bed as soft as a cloud and opened her eyes. No quilted bedspread or pink canopy. No china dolls on the shelf or lacy curtains. This was not her bedroom.

She reached for a lantern to turn it up and found none. Yesterday's events flashed in her mind. Sneaking away to escape that wretched engagement. Planning to stay with Dusty. His face on a wanted poster. The close call at the train station and somehow landing over a hundred years in the future.

None of this seemed real, but it had happened. Actually, she rather liked experiencing the new sense of freedom in this world. Staying out until the wee hours where nobody knew her. No one watching her. No worries about having her escapades being reported back to father.

Red numbers flashed from a box on the nightstand. 5:27. She got out of bed and put on the fluffy robe Kristy loaned her. Slipping out the door, she made her way across the hall to the washroom and sat on the commode, staring at a curtain with a grizzly bear tucked into the bathtub. A giggle bubbled out, and she covered her mouth. She finished her business and headed out the door.

"What's so amusing this early in the morning?" Zack stood outside the bathroom door surprising her.

"The bear curtain."

"Kristy found it at a swap meet. It is unique," he chuckled. "I 'm gonna make coffee. Why don't you join me in the kitchen?"

"That sounds divine." It wasn't like she would be able to go back to sleep. "Give me a few minutes to dress, and I'll be there."

She wore the jeans from last night along with a maroon-colored waist shirt and the pair of cowboy boots she'd packed. Searching her bag, she found a blue ribbon near the bottom, grabbed her brush, and tied her hair back. She walked out following the aroma of freshly brewed coffee down the stairs.

"Have a seat." Zack poured them each a cup of coffee. "Cream or Sugar."

"Both please." She sat on one of the tall barstools and spooned two helpings from the small sugar bowl. As far as cream, all she saw was a large container of Cremora. She watched Zack open the lid and used a spoon to add a couple of dollops.

"Help yourself."

She took her spoon and added the powdery substance into her cup and watched it dissolve the moment it hit the liquid. Amazing.

"Care for toast?" Zack grabbed a loaf of bread in a clear wrapper and took out two slices.

"Yes, please."

He put the slices into a metal device. A minute later, the toast popped up, and he buttered the slices, handed her one on a napkin, and settled on a stool next to her.

"What are your plans for today?"

"I had hoped to find my brother." Not that she had a chance in hades of that happening here.

"I texted my friend that used to work at Los Flores last night." He picked up his phone. "Nothing so far. Do you need a ride home?"

Dash it all, she had no home. "I am not sure. Maybe just a ride to a hotel." She clasped her fingers together.

"I have to work later tonight, so I could drop you off then,"

"I suppose," she said without giving him a definite yes or no.

"I need to feed the horses. Why don't you take a walk with me?"

ZACK LED her into the stables with his dog trotting at his side. "Tell me more about your brother. What was his job at Los Flores?" His voice sounded almost terse and rather serious.

"Foreman."

"Interesting. I'm pretty sure the foreman's name is Robert."

"I must be mistaken about where he worked." She worried her bottom lip. He'd mentioned last night that he knew people at the ranch. What if he learned Dusty had never worked there—at least not in this century?

"Hmm ..." He opened the top of the half-door, and a beautiful nutmeg horse pushed her head over. "Hello, Queenie," he brushed his hand down the mare's nose. Reaching in his pocket, he held up a carrot in his palm. "That's a good girl."

"Is she a Morgan?" Josie rubbed the horse's neck.

"Good eye. Most people think she's a quarter." His lips quirked up. "You ride?"

"As often as I'm able." Which made her miss the pretty palomino she'd left behind. The dog moved to her side, and she patted his head. "What kind of dog is Duke?"

"Black lab."

"He's pretty friendly."

"Yeah. Duke's my pal." He whistled, and the dog went to his side. "I've got to muck out some stalls. We can go for a short ride afterward." He put a halter around Queenie and tied her outside to a hitching post. "How's that sound?"

"Wonderful." The idea of riding filled her soul with joy. "Would you like some help?"

"Cleaning manure. Really? It's pretty messy."

"I've done it before with my brother. I don't mind." At her grandfather's ranch, everyone was expected to help out including her. She'd learned to be responsible and in the process learned to be useful. Productive. Needed.

His grin deepened. "That would be great. Grab some rubber boots. There's an extra pair along the wall." He motioned toward the left side on the floor.

She slipped a pair on over her cowboy boots. Thank goodness she had thought to pack them. Handed a pair of leather gloves, she began shoveling heaps of dung and depositing the waste into a wheelbarrow. She doubted her father had ever cleaned out a stall, relying on staff to do what he called *"dirty work,"* but Josie found the task relaxing.

"You don't mind doing this?" Zack swept the floor.

"You act surprised."

"I am. Although I'm not complaining."

"Do you own all the horses on this property?"

"My uncle owns most of them, but we're also boarding about ten." They finished one stall and spread straw on the bottom. He untied Buttercup's reins from the post and brought a spirited filly into her stall.

"I've got to ride her."

"She likes to ride hard. I think one of the other mares would be better for you."

"No. I mean," she softened her tone. "I would much rather take Buttercup unless she belongs to someone else."

"Persistent, aren't you?" Zack let out a throaty laugh. "My uncle purchased Buttercup for my aunt, but she prefers her pinto. We have considered selling her."

As if knowing Buttercup were aware, they talked about her, she put her head over the door and let out a snort.

Josie rushed over to the mare and rubbed her nose. “Don’t let Zack’s words worry you. I think you are really special,” she crooned to the horse.

The horse whinnied.

“You definitely have a way with her.”

“Thus, you’ll let me ride her.” She had this compelling desire to win him over.

“We’ll see.” He winked.

As they continued working, she found herself humming.

“Oh Susanna, huh.” Zack asked causing her to startle. He sang along. Unlike Garrett who made her all tingly inside, Zack reminded her of Dusty. Kind and calm.

“Garrett says you’re a pretty bad pool player.” He gave her a sideways glance.

“It was my first attempt.” She swung her head, and her ponytail hit her cheek.

“No need to get testy,” he chuckled. “It looked like you and Garret hit it off.”

Her cheeks blazed thinking about Garrett. Not about to admit that no other man had ever looked at her like he did, causing her whole body to buzz, she added another load of manure into the wheelbarrow hoping to avoid any more probing.

“We’re done. Let’s clean up, and we can take that ride.”

They removed their rubber boots and left them by the wall, set the gloves on a hook, and washed their hands at a basin outside.

"You sure you can handle Buttercup? We've got some tamer mounts."

"Don't worry about me. My grandfather set me atop a pony when I was three. I graduated to horses when I was seven." Excitement had thrilled through her whole boyd as her grandfather booted her up.

"If I find she's too much for you, you're off. Understand?" His direct stare said he meant business.

"It won't be necessary, I promise." The fact that he cared about her welfare warmed her soul. She wasn't sure how much she should trust him, nonetheless she believed he might eventually become a friend.

"Fine. Think you can manage bringing her to the hitching post?"

"Of course." She got Buttercup.

Zack brought out a saddle and started saddling the mare.

"I can do that. Go ahead and get your horse."

CHAPTER 13

Josie clicked Buttercup into a gallop behind Zack and gazed out at the farmland. Rows and rows of leafy green crops filled a large fenced-off section of a field. "Is that alfalfa?"

"Good eye. We grow our own stock and sell any extra bales."

"What's that machine over there?" It looked like a green monster.

"A flail chopper. It cuts off the tops of the crop. We've got another machine that gathers."

Her grandfather would have loved the idea of these timesaving inventions.

"We're going to the ranch across the street. I want to check out the new stallion Garrett's brother just purchased."

They trotted down a path that divided the crops

from the fenced fields. A pair of colts frolicked near a copse of trees.

"Looks like you have some spirited colts."

"That's Jack and Daniel named after their sire Whiskey Runner," Zack chuckled.

"Cute pun." She had to admit she liked his sense of humor.

"When we reached the iron gates, we'll leave Fairfield Farms. I'll let you out, and you can wait on Buttercup near the berm at the side. We'll cross Buckshot Road together." Zack hopped down and opened the latch and shut the gate behind them. The soft sound of water lapped against the river's shore several hundred yards to the east. She wished they'd moved closer so she could see if it was the same river where she and Dusty had swam.

"Go home, Duke," he called, and his dog took off toward the house.

"How'd you get him to do that."

"Like I said, he's a good dog."

A car drove by. The noise made her flinch, and she pulled back on the reins. The horse danced to the side. "Sorry, girl." She sucked in a deep breath. Would she ever get used to so many changes in the future?

"Are you okay?"

"Yes," she didn't mean to bark, but heck, the last

twenty-four hours were extraordinary. Bizarre. Crazy.

"Let's cross." They rode a few yards further when she spotted a metal sign swinging back and forth with the breeze as it hung the entrance beam. Two *S's* intertwined with a silver spur. It looked just like the sign she'd helped her grandfather craft for this ranch.

This couldn't be. She blinked several times and looked again. "Is this the Silver Spur Ranch?"

"You've been here before?" His brow rose.

Yes, she wanted to say, but that had been over a hundred years. "The property once belonged to my-my ancestors."

"It must've been a long time ago. Garrett's family has owned this ranch for about fifty years."

"Well … my family lost it in 1885." Her hands tightened around the bullhorn. How could she be in the same place where she'd spent at least a dozen summers?

"Wow. This is quite a coincidence. What made you recognize it?"

"I saw a sketch of the sign." Close enough to the truth she thought. Since she'd been the one to originally come up with the design.

"It must have been really old."

"Ancient history."

"This is all so weird. You know it's almost like you and Garrett are related."

Was she attracted to a distant relative? An ache balled up in her stomach.

"Chill, Josie. What I meant is you're most likely related by land not blood." Zack actually smirked. "Was their last name Smith like you?"

She nodded and looked away.

Half a mile down the road they passed a chicken coop. Her lips twitched slightly at the corners visualizing her grandmother tossing feed to the chickens. As they continued, she spotted a gable roof. This used to be such a special place. Overcome by memories, she lowered her head, and a tear rolled down her cheek. She kneed her mare to a canter, veered past a field with several horses and then toward a sizable building. The building had been painted forest green instead of beige, but the structure was the same as it had been when grandfather held her hand and showed her it. *"Horses will always be an important part of your life, Jo Jo. Treat your horse with kindness, and you'll never be disappointed."* Her grandfather taught her to respect all animals.

They got off their mounts, tying their horses on the fence. She rubbed her hands against the metal siding. Inside an arena, a man worked a tall gray steed around scattered barrels.

"Josie watched the horse maneuver the course with ease. "Whoever thought of using barrels is a genius."

"You ever race them?"

"Never." Although it did look fun. "How about you?"

"No. Fairfield Farms keeps me busy enough." His brief wince morphed into a smile as they moved to a fenced in arena. "There's Garrett's brother."

"Hey, Zack," A man in a Stetson brought his horse to the railing and dismounted. The men shook hands.

"Tyler, this is Josie Smith. She's tagging along today."

"Nice to meet you." Tyler looked like a stocky, darker-haired version of Garrett.

"That horse is impressive."

"Thanks. It's taken a lot of practice to get him there." Tyler puffed up, standing a little taller. "Do you guys wanna see our new stallion?"

"You bet," Zack said.

Tyler led them several yards further to a coral where a black stallion who pranced as he showed off his white sock markings.

"He's got nice lines," Josie said. "How does he ride?

"Like a dream. You seem to know your horses. Where you from?"

"Granite Heights."

"But her family once owned this ranch. Isn't that interesting?" Zack rubbed his hands together.

"Sorry to hear you lost this property. I love it here."

"It was a long time ago."

"Over a hundred years," Zack chimed in. "What are the odds that Garrett and I would meet Josie at the Founders Day Celebration?"

"Probably a million to one." Tyler shook his head. "Is that why you're here today?"

"She wasn't even aware I live next to the Silver Spur. After helping me clean out the stalls, I took her for a ride." Zack quirked an eyebrow at her. It almost seemed as if he knew she was at a loss for words, knew she needed rescuing.

"Let's head over to the house. April's into history. She won't want to miss out on any of the details."

In a few minutes she'd get to see her grandfather's farmhouse.

"Works for me. I'd like to talk with you about considering breeding Sophia or Beatrice with your new stallion. They'll both be in heat soon."

"Sounds good. We can work out a schedule over coffee."

The group mounted their horses. Instead of moving south toward the farmhouse, they went northeast and arrived at a smaller home less than a mile from the street. She tied her horse at a hitching post and followed the men up two flat white steps into the residence.

"I'm home," Tyler called. A blur of red and yellow stripes sailed into Tyler's arms. "Whoa there, partner." With tenderness in his eyes, he beamed at a little boy.

Josie glanced around the open space and focused on a rock fireplace filling the back wall. A marble mantle with a dozen photographs in frames. Family photos with smiling faces. Don't tear up, she told herself, but it was hard to fight with the homey atmosphere here. Even the dark brown leather and matching sofa top with dozens of colorful pillows facing the hearth gave a comfy and welcoming feel.

A woman stood on the other side of the counter separating the living room from the kitchen. Three beeps sounded, and she pulled out a tray with freshly baked muffins. She wiped her hands on her apron, reached over and gave Zack a big hug. "I see you brought company."

"Sure did. April, this is Josie Smith. Her ancestors once owned this ranch."

"That's cool. I'd love to hear all about them." She

picked up a doll from the floor and placed it on the counter. "Let's sit in the living room."

"Honey, we're gonna talk business for a minute." Tyler kissed his wife on the cheek. He went behind the counter, held up a glass pot, asked who wanted coffee, and passed them out before heading over to the dining room table near the back with Zack.

April moved to the couch and pulled a toddler on her lap.

Josie eased into one of the leather chairs. "Your son is adorable."

"Noah's also quite a handful." The corners of April's mouth twitched up. "How'd you meet Zack?"

"At the Founder's Day Celebration. It's a funny story. Garrett mistook me for someone else and threw me in jail." Mercy. She could feel her cheeks heat at the mention of that man.

"For the fundraiser?"

"Exactly. At the time, I thought there had been a terrible mistake. How could any believe I committed a crime. Later on, Garrett apologized." Bought her lunch. Danced with her. Taught her to play pool.

"I'm sure he did. Garrett's a good guy."

They talked about her staying overnight at the bunkhouse and discussed her history with the Silver Spur.

"Why haven't you ever been here before?"

"I learned about this place when I was little but never thought much about it, until I saw the sign above the entrance." She bit her bottom lip and looked down. "For some reason, the brand had stuck with me as did the year my ancestors lost the ranch."

"That's amazing. Do you have any old photos?"

"I have no idea. My-my aunt kept everything with her, and she's passed away." Yeah, right. Keep up with the lies, and her nose would start growing.

"That's too bad. Anyway, I'd love to give you a tour. How long will you be at the bunkhouse?"

"I'm not certain." As if Josie had any idea. She'd be lucky to stay another night. She glanced toward the door. Something about the painting captured her. She stared at the landscape of a meandering river with two men galloping along the shoreline. Her picture of Dusty and Gramps. The one she created shortly before her mother disappeared. Gramps had been so impressed with her work that he'd cut up a board, framed it, and hung it on the wall. She had to blink hard to keep from crying. "Where did you find that painting?"

"In the attic of the old farmhouse where Tyler's grandmother lives. I'd gone up there to look for furniture for the nursery and found it stacked against the wall." She bounced the baby in her lap.

"It's signed by J. Goodwin. Have you ever heard the name?"

"Yes, I believe I have," she said.

"The artist is quite talented. I've been meaning to try and research him or her, but … well, these two keep me hopping."

Zack moved behind her chair in the living room. "Ready to head back."

"Yes." Walking toward the door, she couldn't help flinching when she looked at the painting. Her painting. It somehow felt wrong to have it hung here when its home had been in the living room of her grandfather's ranch.

"What's wrong?" he asked when they got outside.

"It's been strange coming here."

"I think we should talk," Zack said.

Land sakes. That didn't sound good. Not at all.

CHAPTER 14

Zack had been quiet during the ride back to Fairfield Farms "There's a bench near the river where we can have a conversation without being overheard."

What did he know about her? She told herself not to panic, but her heart thudded against her chest so hard she thought it might breakthrough. They slowed their horses under a huge oak tree and let the animals graze on the rich grass. Perching herself at the edge of a bench, except for the huge poles with wires draped between them, Surprise Valley looked much like it had during her time. She used to ride Duchess across the narrower section of the winding river.

Zack sat next to her. "I think you're keeping a secret."

"Whatever do you mean?" She pressed her lips together.

"There's something different about you. Tell me the truth, was yesterday the first time you ever rode in a car?"

"Does that matter?"

"Yes."

Well, she had ridden in a carriage countless times. That should count.

"Fine. I'll take your silence as a yes." He crossed his arms. "You got twitchy when you heard Kristy talking on speaker phone. That's because you've never used a cell phone."

"What are you implying?" she asked.

"Nothing. I want to help you, but you have to be honest. I saw how your face turned pale when you saw that painting near the door. It means something to you."

"I thought it was pretty." She avoided making direct eye contact.

"What about the way you flinched when you mentioned losing the ranch in 1885?

She gulped, swallowing hard.

He put his hand over hers. "Are you a time traveler?" his voice stayed even, controlled.

"What do you mean?" Her foot made a circle in the dirt.

"I have a feeling you are from the 1800's. I think you somehow stumbled through a portal into the future."

She closed her eyes. Should she admit to something she herself didn't understand?

"It's okay. I get it."

"You do?" She bit her bottom lip, not quite certain what to think.

One side of his mouth tipped up. "It happened to me."

She lifted one finely arched eyebrow and stared at him. "You're from the past?" A chill shivered up her arms.

Zack let out a long sigh. "One minute I was riding a locomotive in 1887, the next I landed in modern-day Whiskeyville." Zack stopped talking as if allowing her to process what he'd said.

The world seemed to stop. A hammer pounded against her temples, making her head hurt. It was too much. "This doesn't make sense."

"You're telling me?"

She sucked in deep breaths. In and out. "Are there others like us?"

"Not that I know of."

"Why did this happen to me—to us?"

"I have no idea. I guess we're just lucky." His shoulders lifted.

Josie covered her face with her palms and let out the breath she had been holding. "What am I going to do? I have no money. No place to live. No family." The whole ordeal tumbled through her brain. She needed to take in everything she just heard, needed a plan.

I had one. Look where it got me.

"I'll help if I can." He placed his hand over hers. "But you're gonna need to trust me."

As if she had any other choice. Could she trust this man? A practical stranger. He had been nothing but kind Still, her brain struggled to understand what just happened.

"Stay at the bunkhouse. You'll be safe."

Safe. Would she ever feel safe in this outlandish new world? "I can't stay here forever. I mean it's one thing to put me up for a night, but—"

"We'll take it one day at a time and figure this out together." He squeezed her hand.

What other options did she have? She shrugged. Zack was a time traveler just like her. If she decided to have faith in anyone, it should be him. Deep in her soul, she knew he would assist her. "You're a nice man."

"Shh. I don't want that getting out," he snickered.

She released some of her pent-up tension. "How did you end up living at Fairfield Farms?"

"Actually, I had been on my way to work at my aunt and uncle's farm when I got off the train. I must've walked for hours before Kristy found me and brought me into the house. And her parents took me under their wing."

"So, they know about you?" Each idea seemed to be more and more farfetched.

"Not at first, but yes, they do now. As do Kristy and Garrett." He tweaked her nose. "On that note, I'll talk to those two when we get home." He gave her an intent look. "I'll even try and find you a way back if you'd like."

"Have you ever attempted to return to … where are you from?"

"Cedar Springs."

"I know that town. Dusty took me there. The general store has the best gumdrops."

"Old Man Smith used to sneak me butterscotch." He gave a wistful sigh. "But that's been years. Don't get me wrong, I miss my family, but I am much happier in this century. Life is a heck of a lot easier."

Did she want to go back home?

Yes, of course. She understood the expectations and nuances of society in 1890.

But that would mean going back to her father and marrying William.

With her brother on the run, she dodged a bullet arriving here.

And with Zack's help, she should adjust.

"Are you up to riding back now?"

"Certainly." This new century might be the perfect solution to her former dilemma. Whatever happened in this topsy-turvy and upside-down world, she had a new ally, Zack.

CHAPTER 15

Garrett yawned and glanced at the clock. Nine a.m.

One sexy blue-eyed girl invaded Garrett's dreams all night long. How right it felt to have Josie's body pressed against his as they danced. Her jeans clung to her when she leaned over the pool table to take a shot. And that alluring mouth of hers. Damn. He wanted to sample those strawberry-colored lips and see if they tasted as tempting as they looked.

Grabbing a pair of jeans and a clean T-shirt, he headed downstairs and snagged a cup of coffee from the pot Zack had made when he rose to feed the horses. His stomach grumbled, so he got out a slab of bacon and a dozen eggs and started cooking.

"Something smells good," Kristy strolled up and

helped herself to a coffee, before taking a seat at the counter.

"I'll make enough breakfast for everyone. Is Josie up yet?" He asked without turning and plopped four slices of bread into the toaster.

"Don't know, just got up myself. You two were pretty cozy last night." Kristy lifted a brow.

He shrugged.

"You like her." She leaned on her elbows and gave him a glassy stare.

"I just met her, Kris. And she's leaving today although … I hope she'll stay a little longer." He didn't want her to go. Not yet, anyway.

"You gonna help her find her brother?" her tone softened.

"If I can." Hearing the bacon sizzle, he flipped the strips with tongs. "What are you up to today?"

She tucked a strand of blonde hair behind her ear. "Thought I might take a ride to the river before I head for work."

"No shift for me, thank God." He grabbed a paper towel, set slices of bacon on a plate, cracked eggs, added milk, and scrambled the eggs before pouring them into the pan with some of the leftover grease.

"Lucky dog. Think you could give me a refill of coffee?"

Garrett topped off her cup.

The front door opened with Josie laughing and flipping her long ponytail behind her. Zack placed his hand on the small of her back acting far too intimate with her.

"You really woke up in a water trough?" Her face lit up. Her cheeks full of pink.

"Yep. Not one of my finer moments," Zack said. "Taught me tequila's not my friend."

Josie's eyes collided with Garrett's. Her smile dropped, and he had no idea why.

"What were you guys doing?" Garrett asked, determined to act nonchalant.

"Josie helped me out in the stables. She even mucked out stalls." Zack headed for the kitchen and grabbed himself a cup a coffee. "Want one, Josie?"

"Sure," she moved onto a barstool next to Kristy.

"As far as I'm concerned, since she's such a hard worker, she can stay as long as she wants." Zack set a steaming cup on the counter in front of Josie and took the chair to the left of Kristy.

"You'll do anything to get out of doing your chores," Kristy laughed.

"You know me too well."

"Who wants bacon and eggs?" Garrett asked.

Everyone nodded. He scooped up eggs and three slices of bacon and handed Josie a plate, then Kirsty, Zack, and himself.

Garrett sat to the right of Josie. “How are you?”

“Well.” Her eyes didn’t flicker like they had last night. If she got up as early as Zack, she must be tired.

“I took Josie riding over to the Silver Spur this morning,” Zack blurted. “Her family used to own it.”

“That must’ve been a long time ago. My grandfather bought it in the seventies.”

Josie stopped eating and pressed her lips together. Something was up with her. “About that?” her voice hitched, and then there was silence.

“Go on,” Zack nodded at her. “It’s okay you can tell them. Remember, Kristy and Garrett know about me.”

She picked up her napkin and folded it in fourths. “When my grandfather passed, our family lost the ranch … in … 1885.”

“What? Did you just say 1885?” Kristy combed her fingers through her hair.

“I did. What’s even stranger is I-I boarded a locomotive in 1890.” Her fork fiddled with in her eggs. “And stepped off in this century.”

“You’re a time traveler like Zack?” Kristy chimed in, her fingernails tapping the counter. “I thought it was a fluke when Zack came here, but now there’s two people who somehow took a portal into the future.”

Garrett stared at Josie who seemed to shrink in the chair. The lively and cute woman he had been drawn to was from the 1800's. She was different in so many ways, but last night she just seemed fun and flirty. Like a normal woman. Well, she was all woman, just one who was born over a hundred years earlier.

"In a way, coming here is an answer to my prayers." Josie twirled her spoon around her coffee cup.

"Why is that?" Over the shock, well sort of, Garrett's blood still pulsed through his veins like he was waiting for a green light at the starting line of a drag strip.

"Hmm … it's not a great story." She focused on her hands.

"You can't leave us hanging," Kristy said, "spill."

"My father betrothed me to a man I-I do not care for." She went back to stirring her coffee, the circles getting faster and faster. "So I ran away hoping to stay with my brother."

"No wonder you freaked when I said your dad wanted you retained." The pieces were falling together.

"I couldn't help getting upset."

"Still, I'm sorry." He could see her in the jail cell,

her hands trembling when he'd mentioned her father. Now he felt like a heel.

"You didn't know." A wisp of a smile creased the corner of her mouth, and she squeezed his hand. A spark shouldn't be shooting where their fingertips touched.

"An arranged marriage. That's just wrong." Kristy scrunched her eyes.

"I agree, however, this type of pact is not uncommon in my time. One of my classmates married an older man when she was only fifteen and in love with the neighboring boy," she sniffed. "Before we go on, I have one more confession to make."

"What is it?" Kristy clapped her hands. "Let me guess. You robbed a bank? Or maybe sang in a saloon?"

Josie giggled. "Nothing that drastic. My sir name is Goodwin, not Smith"

"I get it. You didn't want your dad to find you." Garrett longed to pull her into his arms. "

"True. However, I do not care to lie."

That comment sucker-punched him. Not like his ex who declared her undying love … until he got injured.

"What are you going to do now?" Kristy asked.

"I told her she could stay a couple of days. Is that okay with you guys?"

Her eyes looked lost, so Garrett gave her a reassuring smile.

Kirsty got up and hugged Josie. "I'm glad you're here with us."

CHAPTER 16

Josie had an ally who'd been through the same crazy journey—and friends she could trust.

"I'm gonna turn on the game. Do you like baseball?" Garrett asked Josie. All he had to do was gaze at her, and she got all fluttery inside.

"Is it anything like stickball?"

"Why don't you sit a little closer, and we can compare notes?" There came that devastating grin.

My goodness, she found his request hard to resist and scooted over allowing a couple inches between them. They were so close she could see the scruff on his chin.

He clicked a small item with buttons, and the black screen on the wall came to life inside the frame. More detailed than any painting.

"This is amazing. It looks like a window to the

world that keeps changing."

"I guess." Garrett chuckled.

A four-inch batter, dressed in a white uniform and a royal blue cap, tapped a white square with his bat, bent his knees and held his bat upright near his ear. The scene zeroed in on a man gripping a baseball. He spit, turned sideways and threw the ball. The image magically switched to the batter who swung and missed.

"I don't understand how people can get into that black frame."

"I thought the same thing when I first saw a television. Those people are actually in another city. Somehow through modern technology and a special camera, we are able to watch this game." Zack gave her an endearing grin.

"What a wonderful concept."

"You're so cute." Kristy scrunched up her nose. "I take simple things like a TV for granted. But the whole concept is pretty cool."

"I wholeheartedly agree." Josie sighed and sank back against the couch.

"We're rooting for the Cheetahs. They're the ones wearing orange and black." Garrett leaned forward. "C'mon pitcher, give 'em a mean curve."

"Or you could pick the Bluebirds like me," Kristy smirked.

Garrett winked at Kristy. "Been a Cheetah's fan since before you were born."

"Like one year makes you ancient." Kristy lifted a shoulder.

"Bases loaded." A man's voice resounded through the room. "Strike two."

"Who's speaking?"

"The announcer. He's in a booth at the game in northern California," Zack explained.

"I forgot you'd never seen a television before." Garrett put his hand on her knee, and my-oh-my electrical charges shot up her leg. "What do you think of it?"

"I find the device fantastical."

"Fantastical?" He inched closer and set his arm across the back of the couch. "You're cute."

"Thank you." Josie had been called beautiful before, but the cute comment made her think of kittens and puppies and everything good. She fought the urge to sigh and sink back into his arms.

"Think our pitcher will throw a knuckleball or slow pitch?" Garrett said to Zack.

"Whatever he does, better not make it a fastball."

The pitcher threw the ball. The batter swung.

"Whitefield's against the back wall. Looks like it's gonna airmail over the fence," the announcer's voice boomed. "Home run."

Zack grumbled, "I said no fastballs."

"Say it louder next time," Garrett gave a throaty chuckle.

"Go, Bluebirds." Kristy clapped her hands.

"Shut up." Zack glared at his cousin.

Josie enjoyed their razzing.

"Anyone want a beer?" Garrett got up, and she couldn't help gawking at how his T-shirt stretched across his broad chest. My goodness, the man could tempt a saint.

"Sure," Zack said.

"Wine for you, Josie?"

"Water is fine." Her mind was already spinning from her crazy morning, and she didn't need a foggy brain.

"I'll take iced tea, please." Kristy reclined in her chair.

Six huge horses filled the screen pulling a wagon. "Are those Belgium drafts? One of the neighboring farms used a draft to plow his fields."

"Actually, they're Clydesdales. The breed comes from Scotland." Zack spouted obviously knowing some horse facts.

"They're magnificent." She scrunched her eyes and read the name displayed on the screen. "You men drink Budweiser. Is it because you appreciate the horses?"

Garrett burst out laughing. "Not at all. We happen to like the taste. Maybe over time you'll change your tune."

"We'll see." If she could stay here indefinitely anything was possible.

Zack rose from his chair. "I've gotta get ready for work unless ... you think I should call in?"

"Call in?"

"Take the night off."

"That's not necessary." Zack had already gone out of his way to help her. She didn't want to make his life any more difficult.

"We'll be fine," Garrett's voice deepened. "Since I'm not working tomorrow, wanna take a ride along the riverbank?"

"Of course." Exhilaration zinged through her brain. She wanted a closer look at one of her favorite places.

"Let her ride Buttercup. She's already proved she can handle the mare," Zack said.

Josie couldn't help launching herself toward Zack and hugging him tightly. "You're the best." Not usually so impulsive, she let go of Zack and glanced at Garrett. The corners of his mouth quirked down. He must've noticed her staring at him because he flashed her a reassuring smile.

CHAPTER 17

The next day, Garrett raced Josie along the riverbed with her in the lead. Her braid flung straight back from the motion. Leaning forward, he squeezed his thighs and clicked his stallion to go faster.

She turned her head, and her lips twitched into a delighted smile.

The thumping in his chest had little to do with the elation of riding like the wind and more to do with her. He had to admit, Josie was magnificent astride a horse.

They reached a sandbar where an oxford lake formed on their side of the river. She reined her horse to stop. “I won!” she shouted, jumping down.

“Only because I gave you an edge.” He dismounted next to her.

"Take that back, Garrett." His name rolled from her oh-so-tempting mouth. The mouth he'd dreamed about kissing. "I won fair and square."

"I suppose you did. Guess that gives you bragging rights."

"I find it impolite to boast."

"But you'd like to, right?" He teased. "And I bet you will when you see Zack and Kristy."

"Then you don't know me very well."

"Nope." Did he really want to know her better? Not at the moment. He'd rather kiss her.

"I recognize this spot. My brother brought me here to swim. The pool isn't as deep or wide now as it used to be, although the oak tree on the other side of the river has become enormous." She let out a long breath.

"Did you swim often?" He pictured her in a skimpy bikini. Water rolling down her bare stomach. His body stiffened. *Get your mind out of the gutter, Garrett.* Back then Josie would've worn a one-piece that went down to her knees, maybe her calves.

"Not enough. And rarely at home. Father forbade me to journey to a nearby lake. He'd said it was unladylike for a woman to cavort in such a manner. Mother thought his ideas were nonsense and brought me to the shore when father was away on business." She looked at the ground. "I apologize. I didn't mean to ramble."

"Don't mind." He bumped his shoulder against her. "Take off your shoes and roll up your pants. We're going wading."

A blush tinged her cheeks. "All right." She slipped off her boots.

He didn't know why seeing her tiny feet caused desire to flair.

She rushed into the water. "Are you coming?"

"You bet." With his pants turned up to his knees, he joined her, reaching a spot where the water tickled his ankles.

She leaned down and scooped up a handful of liquid. Water doused her face and dripped along her neck and inside her blouse, giving him a glimpse of the outline of her breast. "Why are you staring?"

"Because you're pretty."

"My face is up here," she motioned to her eyes.

"You caught me, but to be fair, I was following the line of the water."

"You're impossible."

A splash of water hit him square in the chest.

"If you wanted me to take off my shirt, all you had to do was ask." He tugged off his T-shirt and threw in onto the shore, all the while watching her gaze at him. Her focus wandered from his abs to his chest to his face, and her cheeks became rosy pink. "Like what you see?"

"Um ..." She looked away.

"I'll take that as a yes." Heat crept up his spine, not only from the temperature outside but from the way she'd checked him out. He moved deeper into the pool and dunked under in an attempt to cool down this crazy attraction he had for her. When he resurfaced, he called, "Come join me. The water's perfect."

"Maybe next time."

If he followed his impulse, he'd be picking her up caveman style and watching her sputter as she sank into the water. Her soaked blouse invisible and outlining her boobs. *Whoa! Don't even go there.*

She cupped her hands, drenching her face with water. "This is refreshing."

"I've got a blanket in my saddlebag. We might as well sit on it and dry off."

"Sure."

He walked to his horse, glancing sideways and noting every curve and muscle of her petite body. God, she's sexy. Opening his saddlebag, he snatched the blanket. "If I'd thought this through, I would have packed a picnic. At least I have bottles of water and a couple of power bars."

"What's a power bar?"

He spread out the blanket on a grassy knoll not far from the river. "It's kind of like a cookie except it has extra protein that's supposed to give you energy."

"It sounds sweet, so I'll have to try one." She sat, and he moved in next to her, handing her the bar.

She struggled with the wrapper.

"Allow me," he tore the corner.

"You're too kind."

Kind. She might as well be putting him in the friend's zone.

"This is tasty, although not as good as snicker-doodles fresh from the oven."

"My Aunt Mickie owns a bakery. I'll stop by and pick up some cookies next time I'm in town."

"Would you?" She looked at him like he were her hero, and a piece of him wished it could be true.

"Of course." After that admiring gaze, he'd do just about anything she asked.

"You are the best." One arm looped around his neck. Warm lips pressed against his cheek long enough to allow her floral scent to linger in the air. Her eyes danced with mischief or maybe happiness as she grinned at him with the enticing mouth that drove him mad.

Unable to resist touching her, he traced his

thumb along her lips, finding them as smooth as velvet. “So pretty.”

“Thank you,” she said low and husky.

Heat jolted straight to his lower extremities.

“You said your family owns the Silver Spur. Do you know if my grandfather’s house has changed much?”

“I think it’s the original structure, but it’s been modernized.”

“Oh.” She gazed at him with a hint of sadness. “I know it’s silly, but I assumed it would look exactly like I remembered. I have to accept things change over time.”

“That’s part of life.” The lamebrain idea spilled from his mouth.

“I’d still like to see inside.”

“Another day. I’ll have to get a key from Tyler. I’ve never needed one before. Whenever I go there, usually someone is home.”

“I understand.” Her brows scrunched together. “This is out of the blue, but since your family owns the Silver Spur, why don’t you live on the ranch?”

“When I moved back, I lived in an old cabin with no indoor plumbing that’s miles from the entrance. Then Zack offered me a room, and it was a no brainer.”

“Moved back from where?”

Damn. “Nevada.” He cracked his knuckles. “I used to play on a minor league baseball team.”

“Baseball. Do you mean the game from last night we watched on the television?” She leaned back on her elbows.

“That’s the one.”

“If it’s not too personal, would you mind telling me why you left?”

Yes, he minded. Two years after the accident, the ordeal still played havoc with his brain, but Josie’s expression seemed soft and caring. He realized it was time to get over himself. “I was a catcher. Someone slid into home, and his cleats broke my hand in six places.” He showed her the six-inch red slash that had softened a little from its former angry red.

“That must’ve smarted.”

“You think?” he reached over and cupped her face.

CHAPTER 18

Something big was happening between her and Garrett. Josie sat next to him on a blanket under a tall eucalyptus tree. The moment her eyes met his captivating emerald ones, the intensity made her head dizzy.

Squirrels chittered from the trees and scampered from limb to limb. The river lapped along the shoreline constant while ever changing—similar to Josie's own life.

He lifted his hand, sliding his fingertips across her jawline, tipping her chin up toward him, inciting a white spark of heat through her skin. All the while, his gaze remained glued to hers. His right hand came up and framed her face, angling her to him, leaning in so close she could hear his heart beating wildly, or maybe that was her own.

Her fingers curled into the fabric of his shirt. His mouth pressed against hers. The slightest pressure of his firm lips caused an aching need in her very core. His kiss unhurried as if the world had paused spinning.

"Josie," he moaned her name. "Been dying to do that all day." His mouth was against hers again, teasing her. His hands around her waist, solid and real.

She scooted closer, slipping her arm around his neck.

"You're making me insane."

His touch sparked fireworks inside her while at the same time she felt like she floated on a whisper thin cloud of sensations. "Oh, my goodness."

"My thoughts exactly," he said, his breath warm as he swept his tongue across her lips.

Her mouth opened, and his tongue glided inside. Her initial response to the intrusion should be shock since no man had ever been this brazen with her before, but as his tongue swirled inside her mouth, she melted. Literally. Turning into a wicked mess of yearning. Mingling fully with him, her tongue joined his, tasting him like he were the richest flambee. Scorched and sweet. The dance between them—intimate and delightful and oh-s0-personal. She closed her eyes, drinking in the softness, the nearness, the heat.

His fingers raked through her hair, and he pulled away.

She stared at him, a little surprised that her lips still sizzled from the contact while her pulse ticked against her chest. "T-that was …" Darn if her brain could come up with the appropriate adjective to describe an all-consuming kiss that left her longing for more.

"It sure was." His flushed face proved that the kiss had affected him as well.

Her breath came out uneven.

"You okay?" he took her hand.

"Yes." But she'd be better if he kissed her again.

"I like this spot," He leaned back on his elbows, his gaze connecting with hers as if he could read her every thought. "It's still hard to believe your grandfather once owned the Silver Spur. What was it like back then?"

"The area was quieter. Rather peaceful with more open space and hardly any fences." She pulled her knees up and held them with her arms.

"You said you lived in Granite Heights. How often did you stay out here?"

"Every summer. The day after school ended, my mother and I boarded a northbound locomotive.

Gramps would pick us up at the depot. He always stopped at the general store and bought me a bag of gumdrops." Her mouth watered, recalling the sugary delicacy.

"You like snickerdoodles and gumdrops. Got a sweet tooth, huh?" his deep voice rumbled into a laugh.

"Absolutely. What about you?"

"I've always had a thing for M&Ms. Especially the red ones."

She squinted at him. "What's that?"

My gosh, one little grin from him—even a partial one, and a flash of heat simmered up her arms and settled in her belly.

"Imagine a round chocolate smaller than the size of a marble that's coated with a candy shell. I'll bring home a bag after work tomorrow night."

"That would be lovely." She gazed at him, pleased to learn another layer to this intriguing man. He seemed to like giving gifts.

"It's a deal." He shook her hand. His mouth twisted into a half-grin.

Awareness filled her every pore. The air she breathed seemed to sizzle. Not about to let him see how he affected her, she fiddled with her hands. "What exactly does your job entail?"

"I'm an emergency dispatcher. People call the

station with problems. I listen for details and send out the appropriate agency to their house."

"What do you mean by appropriate agency?"

"We send out fire, police, or ambulances depending on the situation."

"In my time, we had a volunteer fire department and a sheriff and a deputy." She tried to picture this new situation.

"Now, we have dozens of people working in each of the three departments in various capacities. In the call center where I work, there's five to ten people on shift. But you have to remember, there are a lot more people living in this area then in your time."

"It is a lot to fathom. Tell me more about your job. Do you sit or stand?" She tried to picture what that meant.

"I sit at a desk with a computer and phone."

She opted not to ask what a computer might be, deciding to focus on Garrett. "Is the employment difficult?"

"Not really. It can get a bit stressful if someone is having a heart attack or had a car accident, but I'm pretty good as staying calm."

"You do seem to stay even-keeled."

"I try." His shoulder lifted giving her a shrug. "Do you have any hobbies?"

"I like to draw and paint. When I was at your

brother's house the other day, one of my paintings hung near the front door. It was rather odd seeing something I'd once created had survived."

"Is it the landscape with two cowboys riding along the riverbank?"

"That's the one. I painted my brother and grandfather from memory."

"You've got talent."

"Thank you." Once, her mom talked her into entering an exhibit at the fair. She'd won first place, but after mom was gone, she'd lost her drive to compete. Just painted and drew to relax. Refusing to give in to melancholy, she changed the focus to him. "What hobbies do you have?"

"When I'm not riding horses, I like to take out my dirt bike."

"Is that some type of bicycle?"

"It's a motorcycle which is like a bicycle powered with an engine instead of pedaling. I could take you out sometime."

"Oh, yes, please." This world was filled with wonders, and she hoped to experience them all.

"Tell me a secret you have from your childhood."

"Do I have to?" She would prefer not to say anything.

"Come on. I promise I won't tell anyone." He held up two fingers. "Scout's honor."

She clasped her hands together.

"It can't be that bad."

"I suppose not. As a little girl, I … I used to have an invisible friend." The friend first appeared right after she left the ranch. Coming back to her father's home, she had missed her brother, grandparents, and the cowboys at the Silver Spur, so she invented someone to keep her company.

"What was her name?"

"Princess Goodness."

He snickered.

"It's not funny."

"It kinda is." He chuckled, and she found herself laughing along.

"You're right. It is a ridiculous name. But I was only five." She faked a frown. "All right smarty pants, it's your turn. You owe me something embarrassing."

"I had a stuffed dog named Pet. I couldn't go anywhere without him." He gave her an impish grin and she could almost picture him as that cute little boy.

"All right. I don't feel so inane now." She actually liked conversing with him, telling him things no one else ever heard not even her best friend Elizabeth.

"Ready to head back."

"Sure." She helped him fold the blanket.

As soon as he'd stashed it inside his saddlebag, he

called, “Race you to the stables,” he jumped onto his horse.

His words took several seconds to sink in. It seemed like minutes for her to mount and start galloping. She added pressure with her knees to urge Buttercup to go faster but couldn’t catch up to Garrett who was at least a hundred yards ahead.

He met her outside the stables. “What took you so long?” He offered his hand to help her dismount, but she got off the horse on her own.

“You gave yourself an edge.”

“I suppose I did. I like to win.” He grabbed two brushes from inside the stables and handed her one.

“As do I. When I was in primary school, I usually beat my friend racing back from the schoolhouse.” Funny, it seemed liked decades ago since she had been that carefree. Life had been simpler back then. Her only concerns were to keep her grades high and to be a kid.

“Guess we’ve got a competitive edge in common.”

She rubbed down Buttercup and crooned, “You’re beautiful.”

“Actually, I prefer being called handsome or hot,” Garrett joked.

“I was talking to the horse.”

“If you say so.” He strolled next to her and used his finger to tuck a wayward strand of hair behind her ear, and holy moly, her skin scorched where he'd touched. "You need help with your tack?"

"I'll manage." She pushed up the flap of the saddle, unbuckled the girth, and lifted the pad with the saddle off Buttercup's back. She followed behind him and couldn't help noticing how well his jeans molded to his backside. A quiver of excitement shot straight through her body.

CHAPTER 19

Later that evening, Josie sat at the counter. Garrett stood near the stove. They had the house to themselves since both Zack and Kristy were at work. And she didn't mind one bit.

"What are you cooking?"

"Chili dogs." He reached into the icebox, set out a block of cheese and a wrapped package on the counter.

"What's that?"

"A hot dog topped with chili and cheese."

"To be honest, I've only eaten hot dogs at the county fair topped with mustard and ketchup. Although, I do like cowboy chili."

"I'm curious, what used to be in chili in your day?"

"Chuck beef, onion, chili powder, and whatever else the cook decided to throw in."

"I hope this version is okay." His smile was contagious, and she found the corners of her mouth twitching up. "You up for grating cheese?"

"I've never tried it."

"It's not hard." Reaching under the counter, he set a four-sided metal object with various size holes on top of a paper plate. "Slide the cheese downward like this on the medium edge. It collects the pieces in the middle. Your turn." His arm snagged around her waist as he pulled her in front of him.

She breathed in his masculine scent. Her pulse skittered as she skated the cheese wedge up and down. Up and down until all the cheese had been shredded.

He backed away and sliced onion.

Her watery eyes burned like the dickens, and she rubbed them.

He filled a metal pot from the faucet. "How many do you think you can eat?"

"One. Make that two. I am rather hungry."

"Well, I want three, maybe four." Six dogs plopped into the water.

"Where's the fire?" She moved in closer to look at the flame

"There's an electric element in the burner. See the red glow. That's heat."

Heat similar to the blaze his nearness seemed to create. Opting to ignore the charge running through her body, she focused on the stove. "No wood to chop. The scientific advances in this century are simply fascinating."

"I think *you're* fascinating." His arms went to her shoulders, and he pressed a quick kiss on her cheek. He stepped away and opened a can with his hands.

"How'd you do that without a can opener?"

"The lid is precut in the factory," he said with a laugh. "It's fun introducing new things to you."

She found herself warm and not from the stove but from the man. This new strange sensation was what she'd always wanted. A man she desired. One who made her blood surge with want.

"Let's eat." He handed her a plate with two dogs in a bun and fixed his own with three. Spooning chili over the meat, he added cheese and onions.

She copied his actions and sat on a barstool, placing her plate on the counter.

"Want wine or soda to go with it?"

"Sarsaparilla, if you have it."

"One root beer coming up." He slid a bottle across the counter.

"Chips?" He reached his hand into a bag.

"Yes, please."

He put a handful of the snack on her plate.

She picked up a chip and bit into a salty, crunchy potato.

He pulled out the barstool on her right, and his hand brushed her leg as he sat down.

A spark shimmied along her thigh.

"Chili dogs are a main staple in this house. They're fast and filling." Garrett held the bun in one hand, took a bite.

She carefully nibbled on the end of the bun. As hungry as she was, the combination of meat and beans tasted good. Taking another bite some chili dropped on her plate, and she gasped.

"I saw that." His eyes glinted with mischief.

"Oops." She giggled.

They finished their meal and threw their plates in the trash.

"Wanna watch a movie? It's kind of like a play but you see it on TV."

"All right."

"Action or comedy?"

"Comedy." Laughter was the best medicine as far as she was concerned. Once again. She couldn't wait to sit close to Garrett and hoped to steal another kiss.

"If you're too tired, I don't mind taking a

raincheck on the movie. You woke up way earlier than me.

How considerate. When was the last time someone cared about whether she was tired or even happy? Her father was distant and remote. The housekeeper and butler made sure she had what she needed and were almost like family—except they answered to her father, not her. But Garrett seemed to be genuinely interested. "I'm staying right here."

The idea of a movie wasn't what kept her glued to the couch. It was Garrett with his kissable mouth and virile body.

He clicked the television. Tiled rows of photographs appeared. "Dr. Doolittle is about a physician who talks to animals. How does that sound?"

"Perfect."

The movie played. A parrot, gorilla, polar bear, ostrich, dog, and duck had conversations with the disheveled man. "How did they get the animals to talk?"

"It's dubbed in." He snaked his arm around her shoulder and tugged her closer.

"The scene seems so real."

"Uh-huh." He kissed her cheek, his day-old shadow prickly against her skin.

She leaned into him. Enjoying the coziness. As

the movie progressed, she asked, "Have you ever seen a real giraffe or gorilla?"

"At the zoo."

"I read about a zoo in Philadelphia, but I've never been there." She longed to travel the continent.

"The best one is in San Diego. It's about three hours from here." He nibbled on her ear, and energy jolted down her spine. Then he kissed her, just a quick peck. "We've got cookie dough ice cream in the freezer. Would you like a bowl?"

"Of course." She sank into the back of the couch.

"Here you go." His fingertips grazed hers, causing a sizzling spark as he handed her the bowl and sat close to her. He watched her as she took a bite.

"This is delicious. Whoever decided to mix in dough is brilliant."

"Wait until you try cherry jubilee. It's my favorite."

She would store that information for later. Taking another spoonful, the cold, sweet sensation reminded her of a frozen Bavarian cream pudding. In no time, her spoon scraped the bottom.

He leaned over and kissed her. The flavor of ice cream on his tongue. He kissed her for the longest time, causing a crackle of energy between them. Tantalizing. Delicate. Sinfully seductive.

And then he pulled away. "This is nice," he said, holding her in his arms.

Nice. More like fiery and fantastic. Kissing could easily turn into her favorite craving. She had been tempted to pull his mouth back to hers. Instead, she attempted to concentrate on the movie but found it hard to follow with him at her side.

A WARM BODY leaned against Garrett's side on the couch. He opened his eyes. Josie's dark red hair wisped across her forehead, and he couldn't resist pushing the wayward strand behind her ear. Her flawless skin had a splattering of freckles along the bridge of her nose. He ran his fingertips over the specs, and she wiggled her nose and swatted his hand like she might do to a fly.

The front door shut, and she startled, sat up straight and blinked several times. "What-what is going on?"

"Sorry. Just got back from work." Zack strode in.

"We were watching a movie and—well—we fell asleep." Garrett felt the need to explain why he cuddled up next to their house guest.

"What time is it?" Josie stretched her arms above her head.

"After eleven."

"That late." She practically leaped up. "I'm going to retire."

He watched her scurry up the stairs, suddenly missing the closeness they'd shared.

"You guys have a good time?"

"Yep." Garrett's right eye twitched.

"I don't want things to get awkward while we figure out what to do with her." Zack snagged a water from the fridge and sat at the other end of the couch. "It's obvious you like her."

"She's different." And pretty and sexy and fun to be around.

"She's from the 1800s, obviously an innocent. You'd better be careful."

"It's nothing serious." Why did that idea slam hard into his chest? He liked spending time with her … at least for the time being.

"Good. I can relate to her situation. When I first arrived, things were confusing." Zack downed his water. "If I hadn't met the Fairfield's, I don't know what might have happened to me."

"Josie has us. Judging from what I've seen so far, she's got guts. When I arrested her, she handled it, and she was a great sport at the bar. Plus, she knows horses. I think she'll do just fine here." He didn't want her to leave anytime soon.

"I think so, too." Zack punched him in the arm. "But we should come up with a backup plan for her, just in case things go sour with her staying at the bunkhouse."

CHAPTER 20

Friday afternoon, Josie rode in the passenger seat of Kristy's car.

"How's it going with Garrett?"

Leave it to Kristy to say what's on her mind. Exactly how much did her friend know? Was she referring to the fact they'd kissed? Her first real kiss had her lips tingling even now. She had breathed in his woodsy scent as he held her against him. Her fingers gripping his muscular arms.

"I've hardly seen him the last few days." An image flashed in her mind of his lithe body as he raced her astride his tall stallion. At the shore of the river, he'd gazed at her with eyes the color of clover with a hint of mustard in the center, and all logic seemed to go out the door. She knew it was a mistake to get involved given her present circumstance, but the man was mighty tempting.

"As if that matters. You like him, don't you?"

The man oozed allure, plus he had a sweet side. His gift of a sketch pad and combo set of drawing pencils and charcoal set her heart to flutter. "Would that be a problem?"

"Probably not. As long as you're not thinking long term. Garrett's been burned a few times. He's pretty gun shy."

"Oh." Well, she might favor him more than she cared to admit, but she had no idea how long she'd be around. She glanced out the window as they drove into an enormous parking lot with hundreds of cars. She could only see the front side of the rectangular complex with stores named Macy's, Bravo Books, Green Garden Diner, Jacob's Jewelers. Dozens of people strutted toward what appeared to be the main entrance.

Kristy parked in front of a boxy brown building. "Let's start at Kohls. I've got a thirty percent off coupon."

"Even with a discount, I feel guilty letting Zack foot the bill."

"Don't worry. Zack insisted on buying you some things after all of your help especially in the stables. He tends to take on too much, working nights and running the ranch during the day." Kristy's eyes softened. "Consider the clothes part of your salary."

"I appreciate having a place to live. Without you, Zack, and Garrett, I don't know how I would have managed."

"I'm sure you would have survived. You're pretty strong."

Josie had never considered herself strong. She endured her mother's disappearance because what other choice did she have? As far as daily living, everything she needed had been provided.

She stepped in front of a glass door, and it slid open. "That's amazing."

"I've never thought much about automatic doors. With you around, I find myself appreciating little things."

"I like this world."

"You're adjusting a lot easier than Zack did. The first time he heard a tractor startup, he covered his ears and ran for cover."

"That seems so out of character from the man I've seen. He always appears composed and in full control." Zack was a calming influence on her.

"He's gotten better."

"How long has he been at your farm?"

"Hmm ... Three years last March. He just turned twenty-five in May." They walked past a section with women's clutches and handbags. "I'm not complaining. I consider the big lug a brother."

"I miss my brother." Memories flooded her mind. Memories of Dusty's endless patience when she constantly asked him questions about life on the Silver Spur. Memories of him, strong and confident riding his steed.

"It must be hard knowing that you'll never see him again."

"It is." She wiped away a tear and straightened her shoulders, determined to embrace the future.

"We're going to head for the escalator to the junior's section upstairs."

"All right." Josie watched two women walk onto steps that moved on their own accord. Amazing.

Kristy grabbed the handrail and stepped on.

Josie got on and wobbled, holding on to the vibrating handrails for dear life until she got about halfway up, and she let herself relax. Reaching the top, her feet faltered.

Kristy steadied her with a hand. "Sorry. I forgot you've never ridden on an escalator."

"No need to fret. It was fun." She laughed and glanced at a faceless mannequin wearing a frilly pink dress that came above the knee.

"That's cute." Kristy led her to a rack of dresses. "What size are you?"

Heck if she knew.

"I'm an eight. You're probably a four or maybe a six. We'll try both." She reached the center of a rack and plucked two dresses. "Sundresses are on the back wall. Let's see if there are any you like."

"I like everything." And she did. So many ready-made choices. Far better than being fitted by a tailor.

It didn't take long for each of them to have an armful of dresses to try on. "This way."

The fitting rooms had mirrors on two walls. Josie unbuttoned the front of her floral top. Then she tried on the pink dress and twirled. Her entire calf showed. She should be embarrassed to be wearing such a risqué garment, but she wasn't. Not even a little bit.

"Did you find anything you like?" Kristy asked from the room next to her.

"The pink dress."

"Let me see. Come on out."

As Josie stepped out, Kristy clapped. "Perfect."

"I agree. Your dress is pretty but …" Josie didn't want to offend her friend.

"The bright red washes out my complexion. I know this, yet I always gravitate toward this color." Kristy laughed.

Picking out jeans turned out a lot more complicated than dresses. There seem to be hundreds of brands and hundreds of styles. By the time she found jeans that accentuated her derriere it felt like she'd tried on thousands of pants. And she couldn't believe how comfortable and easy to wear undergarments turned out to be. Then they looked at blouses, and skirts, plus high heels, sneakers, and boots. Exhausting. Hectic. Entertaining.

THREE HOURS LATER, Josie left the mall with so many bags filling her arms she could barely see where she was walking.

CHAPTER 21

After five days of work, Garrett finally had a day off to spend with Josie. He rode his motorcycle to the Silver Spur farmhouse with her arms cinched around his waist, making it hard to concentrate. He wanted her. He knew it was wrong. Very wrong. He had no business messing with her.

But that didn't stop him from desiring her.

He parked his bike near the front entrance, and she waited next to him on the porch. Her posture straight, her shoulders back, her mouth pinched together pencil thin. "I should be excited about going inside and seeing this place that meant so much to me. Why do I feel more jittery than a rabbit in a wolf's mouth?"

"A rabbit in a wolf's mouth?" he chuckled and held the door for her.

"My grandfather had an analogy for almost everything. The funny ones stuck in my brain." She passed him in her form-fitted jeans and a tank top.

He sucked in a breath. Damn, she's hot.

"We used to hang our Stetsons on those pegs on the wall." She pointed to a rack not far from the entrance.

"Let me guess yours was pink."

"Brown. It hides dirt."

"Never thought you'd be so practical," he chuckled.

"Believe me, I own plenty of fancy hats."

"Like the blue one you wore when I met you." She was used to having nice things. Just like his ex. Except Josie was nothing like her. Plus, there's no reason they couldn't have fun while she stayed at the bunkhouse.

She went over to the rocking chair and sat. "My grandmother used to sit here darning socks or embroidering."

"It must be weird revisiting your past like this."

"It is." She walked over to the fireplace and ran her hand over the top corner of the redwood mantle. "I can't believe my great-grandfather's initials are still along the edge." Picking up a family photograph with Garrett in it, she asked, "How old were you in this picture?"

"Ten or eleven. Don't judge the bowl cut. Everyone had one."

"I think you look adorable."

"You mean dorky."

She shrugged. "You and Tyler look alike. Your sister and younger brother seem to take after your mother."

"I suppose. What about you and your brother? Does he share your gorgeous blue eyes?"

"His are gray like his father?"

"You had different dads?"

"Dusty's my half-brother."

He took her hand and led her into the kitchen. "As you can see, this room has been modernized. I helped my grandfather put in those stone tiles." He motioned to the gray flooring.

"There used to be wood planking. This is much better than getting splinters in your socks."

"I'm sure it is. Anyway, the countertops are made of granite."

Her fingertips glided along the top. "I like what you've done here. Did you paint the walls grey?"

"One summer my sister and I helped paint the inside of this house."

"Birdie, right? I'd like to meet her."

"Maybe. It's still summer break for her, but she'll be gone soon."

"Kristy said she's a teacher in Colorado."

"Yep. My vagabond sister is off for the summer and has been in California for over a month, but she tends to gravitate to the mountains or the ocean."

"My mother and I used to ride the train to the seashore. I remember collecting seashells." Her voice came out light and bubbly while she bounced on her toes.

God, she was pretty. He cleared his throat and said, "Ready to see the rest of the house?"

"I am."

He brought her to a room near the back and opened the door to a pink disaster. "This is my grandmother's room."

"I adore pink however, even I think this is a smidgeon too much."

"I agree, but Granny loves it. She's on safari in Africa with some friends. Knowing her, she'll be bringing back some weird trinkets to add to her shelves." He shut the door.

"That continent takes months to get to by ship." Her jaw dropped with surprise.

"Yes. Although, people usually take airplanes. You can go almost anywhere in the world in less than a day."

"And here I thought train travel was marvelous."

"It is for the most part. Except travel is kind of a

pain now. You have to get to the airport at least an hour early and go through a security checkpoint. Then you wait to board the plane. But the upside is a trip from California to the East Coast can be completed in six hours."

"How splendid." She scrunched up her face.

He assumed he'd gone over her head with info but liked the way she didn't seem to get flustered.

They moved on to the next room decorated in varying shades of green.

"When I stayed in this room, my bed was covered with a patchwork quilt." Tears pooled in her eyes as she walked inside and sat on the bed. "At night, crickets chirped, owls hooted, coyotes howled, and I'd never been happier."

He reached for her hand and squeezed it.

"Thanks again for bringing me here," her voice came out choked.

"You're welcome." A part of him wanted to pull her into his arms and say everything would be all right. She had been through so much over the past week and had remained as strong as anyone could be given the circumstances. "Let's explore the attic."

"I'd like that." She followed him into the living room and over to a rectangular hatch in the hall.

He yanked on a cord attached to the fold-down stairs. "Does this look familiar?"

"It does. I haven't been in the attic in years."

He grabbed a flashlight from an end table and clicked. The light made her hair shimmer. "I'll go first." Taking several steps, he swept away cobwebs at the top of the landing. Light filtering in from a window helped them navigate inside the space. When he pulled on a string hanging from the ceiling, dust moats danced across the area cluttered with furniture, broken appliances, Christmas decorations, fishing poles, and various stuff.

She moved up next to him, and again, he was reminded how he towered over her. At five-nine, he'd never considered himself tall, but with the petite-sized Josie, he longed to be her protector.

The floor creaked as she sat in an old rocking chair. "Granny loved this chair." Wiping away tears from her eyes, she said, "I'm sure this sounds ludicrous, but being here somehow makes me feel closer to her."

He recalled the closeness he'd shared with his grandfather. Not about to give into sadness, he drifted to a table where vinyl records were neatly stacked and picked up a Glenn Miller album. "What kind of music do you like?"

"All music."

Immediately his thoughts went back to how her hips swayed when she danced at the bar.

She gravitated to a group of boxes in the corner and kneeled. "I think there's something important on the bottom. Help me get to it."

"Sure." He moved boxes of books and photo albums to the side until he reached a reddish-brown chest. "This looks old?" Blowing dust off the top, he coughed.

"It's my grandmother's hope chest," she sighed. "She used to keep it in her bedroom at the bottom of her bed."

"Let's take this downstairs where the light's better." He picked up the chest finding it bulky but lighter than he'd expected. Even with his lame hand, he maneuvered the wooden box to the ground floor and into the living room.

CHAPTER 22

The hinged squeaked as Josie opened the lid, pulled out an embroidered handkerchief and sniffed it. "Granny used to add a drop of rose oil in the chest, but all I can smell is cedar."

"It's better than mothballs."

"I don't know what those are?" She squinted at him and refocused on the chest, lifting out a yellowed lace cloth. "Granny covered our table with this for Sunday dinners. After church, we'd peel apples and make apple pie. She had this way of making everything we did feel special."

"How old were you when she … passed?"

"Thirteen. She caught a chill one winter and never recovered." Josie sucked in a deep breath.

"Loss is hard. My grandfather died two years ago."

The hole in his heart still ached. Garrett had moved back to Surprise Valley for a whole year before his grandfather passed. It irked him that he hardly visited Gramps before he died. Not about to allow his mind to drift in that depressing direction, he checked inside the trunk. "Is that your comforter?"

She plucked it out of the chest and held it against her. "It is. Every patch represents an important person in my life. My grandmother, mother, and I sewed the pieces together. This red checkered material came from one of Dusty's shirts. The pink my baby bonnet. The lace my mother's wedding dress. The denim grandpa's overalls." Tears rolled down her cheeks, and she wiped them away with her hand. "I know they are long gone. I know this is part of my past. I know I shouldn't be crying, but I can't seem to help myself."

He wrapped his arm around her and held her. "There's nothing wrong with showing emotion. Nothing at all." Even the strongest person could break sometimes. He had when he lost his career. Although he'd never shed a tear, he'd wallowed in pity for months. Hell. Longer than that.

"You are a nice man?"

"Nice. Next you'll be calling me a sweetheart," he said with a laugh.

She stopped crying and gazed up at him. "Well you are."

He reached for a box of tissues on the coffee table and handed her a few. "Here you go."

She pulled out a small metal photo with a couple from the chest.

"Who's this?"

"I recognize my mom. That man must be her first husband." Her mother's face beamed. "My gosh, they were so young. Her husband died when Dusty had been about four or five."

"And then she met your dad?"

"From what she said, they met at the general store. He swept her off her feet, literally, and brought her to his large estate in Granite Heights."

"Away from all she knew."

"I think she loved my father, but she didn't like living so far from her parents." Josie sighed and put her hand into the chest.

He flipped through the pages of a bound book. "This looks like a child's writing with some kind of drawing."

He read the words:

July 5th, 1875

I love the 4th of July. We saw fireworks. They were beautiful.

Josie

"THAT'S MY DIARY." She snatched the book from his hand and held the leather against her heart. "I can't believe this survived."

"How old were you when you wrote it?"

"Six." It seemed a little disorientating to be here holding something she'd once treasured. She turned to the front of the book, sat up straighter and a smile graced her face. "My mom bought me this book, so I could record all my adventures at the ranch. I remember feeling so grown up."

She turned to the midpoint and stopped at a drawing of a girl with a puppy. The pages were time-worn and delicate. "Grampa gave me Charlotte for my tenth birthday."

Intricate lines formed the animal. "Look at the details in the face. The button nose, the open mouth with the tongue hanging out. You were talented even then."

"I haven't had a chance to thank you for the art supplies." Her expression softened as she gazed at him.

"It was nothing." A quick stop at Target before work.

"I've been spending my afternoons drawing."

"What did you draw?"

"Well, one of the sketches is of the two of us riding along the river." Her cheeks flushed.

"You'll have to show me later."

"I will."

"Tell me about your dog. What did she look like?"

"She was a cocker spaniel with black and white spots. I loved her from the second I saw her. She used to follow me wherever I went on the ranch." She bit her bottom lip. "Then I brought her back to Granite Hills, and my dad became irate. He said that oversized rat *did not* belong in his home and ended up giving Charlotte to a neighboring farm."

"That's cruel. I mean, I know he's your father, but he sounds like an ass."

"I won't disagree." She flipped to another page in her diary.

He couldn't imagine any man being that malicious. "I had a German Shepherd. Loved that guy."

"What was his name?"

"Buddy."

"Nice name," she said.

"Someday, I'll get another dog. For now, I can pamper Duke."

"He is pretty special," she sighed. "Where did Zack find him?"

"He showed up on the farm one day, and Zack took him in. He's a sucker for strays." His friend had a big heart.

"Like me?"

"And me. He talked me into staying in the bunkhouse. Turned out to be a good thing." A good place to lick his wounds and find a new profession.

She turned to another page and gasped. "I must've written this the last summer I came here."

Dear Diary,

I have only two weeks left at the Silver Spur before we must to leave. I wish we could live at this ranch permanently. Unlike the stuffy mansion that father built, this house is warm and cozy. Mother is much more relaxed, content, and happy here."

"The next week my mom went riding by herself. Her horse came back without her. We searched everywhere but never found any trace of her." Her eyes misted but she refused to give into the threatening waterworks.

He wrapped his arm around her shoulders and

held her close, allowing her to coat his shirt with tears. "That must've been hard. You said she disappeared. Do you think she might have time-traveled like you?

"Hmm …" Her eyes lit with surprise. "It is a possibility. What if she's living in this very year?"

"Then I'd say you're lucky."

"The rest of the pages are empty." She closed the book. "I'm taking my diary with me."

"Of course. You ready to head back now."

She nodded.

"Let's put everything back in the chest, and I'll put it up in the attic."

Placing the comforter on top, she shut the lid. "I wish we could take the chest with us, but we're on your motorbike."

"We'll pick it up when I have the truck." He couldn't resist hauling her against him and kissing her.

CHAPTER 23

An hour later, Garrett sat across from Josie at Taffy's Café.

"Thanks for bringing me inside my grandfather's house. Finding the diary means so much." She seemed a little out of sorts, and he couldn't blame her.

"It must've been weird reading it."

"It's rather bizarre seeing something I wrote over a century ago." She stilled and bit her bottom lip. "The words were proof that I cherished living on the ranch."

"What was the Silver Spur like back then?"

"Open and free. I adored spending time with my grandparents. They taught me to appreciate little things like watching a newborn calf take its first breath or enjoying the colors of dusk."

"Back then, there wasn't much around. Did you ever get lonely?"

"Never on the ranch. The summer days seemed to fly by, and then I'd head back to school with my friends."

"Do you like staying at the bunkhouse?" He had to ask.

"Very much."

"Why?"

"I feel a sense of freedom here." She picked up her menu. "Although I have no reason to complain. In Granite Heights, I lived a life of privilege."

For a moment, he'd forgotten she came from money. She was used to the finer things in life.

Hey, Garrett," Taffy Taylor, the owner of the café said. "Haven't seen you here in a while."

"Nope." Garrett tried not to react. The last time Taffy waited on him, his longtime girlfriend dumped him. Why did he have to think about his ex now? Belinda saw him with dollar bills in her eyes certain he'd be drafted into the majors. When he got injured, she broke up with him at this very table. Dammit. He shook his head.

"What would you like to drink?" Taffy asked Josie.

"Sarsaparilla, please."

"You should make it a root beer float. They'll add

a scoop of ice cream." Garrett said, knowing her fondness for sweet things.

"That sounds delightful."

"Coke for me," Garrett added.

Taffy went to the next table and visited with more of her customers.

Josie held the menu in front of her face and peered over the top. "Which burger is better, the baconator or teriyaki?"

"Baconator hands-down. Just be warned, it's kinda messy."

"I'll take that as a challenge."

Taffy dropped off their drinks.

Josie put a spoonful of ice cream in her mouth. The innocent move shouldn't cause him to stare at her lips or make his cock twitch.

Taffy served their food. "Enjoy."

Josie picked up her knife about to cut the bun in half.

"Don't do it," he called.

"Do what?"

"Cut the bun. Burgers are meant to be eaten with two hands." He demonstrated by picking up his sandwich and taking a bite.

"But this one is twice the size of the one at the Shooting Gallery Grill. I can't even fit it in my mouth."

"Think of it as an adventure."

"Not today." She lifted her chin. "Anyway, you've dripped sauce on your shirt."

He looked down at the line of red near the center and used a napkin to wipe it off.

"My way is better." She cut her burger into four parts and ate one of the pieces. This is delicious."

"I know, right." He dipped a fry in ketchup. "After we're done, wanna stop by my aunt's bakery and get a dozen snickerdoodles?"

"Yes, please." And then there it was, the quirk of her lips and that sensuous mouth driving him insane.

CHAPTER 24

Josie rode on Buttercup next to Garrett, Kristy, and Zack as they headed underneath the entrance for the Silver Spur Ranch. She caught herself fiddling with her reins. In a few minutes, they'd be at a barbecue where she'd meet Garrett's family for the first time.

She wanted his parents to like her.

Zack's dog ran alongside the horses until he spotted a squirrel, barked at the critter, chased it up a tree, then sat there bewildered.

"Duke." Zack whistled, and the dog moseyed back near his horse. "He'd sit there all day if I didn't call him."

"That sounds like him." After three weeks at the farm, she'd come to love the Labrador retriever.

Glancing behind an enormous oak tree, she

spotted a red barn. "My grandfather kept a cow named Bessie there," Josie called. "My mom taught me to milk her in one of the stalls."

"In overalls with your hair in braids, right?" Garrett's deep voice shouldn't cause heat to shimmer up her neck and sear her cheeks, but it did.

"Mom said I looked darling," she said, listening to Buttercup's hoofs prodding. "You know, I've been on this property several times now and haven't seen many cattle. Does this ranch still have stock?"

"We have a little over a hundred head. My brother prefers breeding horses."

"You remember seeing that stallion with me the first morning you were here?" Zack asked.

"I do. When do you plan to breed him with Beatrice?"

"Next week."

"That's great. With the mare's sleek lines and the stallion's quarter horse stock, the foals should make good cutters." She could picture a newborn with its spindly legs.

"I can smell the steaks from here." Zack clicked his horse faster. "Think Birdie will make it today?"

"Nope. She went hiking in Big Bear."

"That's too bad. How much longer will she be in California?" She'd swear Zack's eyes flickered with disappointment. Could Zack be interested in Garrett's sister?

"She's leaving next week. I think I saw her for two or three hours the whole time she's been here." Garrett turned to Josie.

"You must miss her."

"We all do," Kristy cut in. "But she seems happy. That's what matters."

"What's Birdie like?" Josie's curiosity had been piqued.

"She's fun. Always joking around," Kristy said.

"And bossy. She's a year younger than me, but that doesn't stop her from thinking she knows everything." The corners of his mouth twitched upward.

"What do you think of her, Zack?" Josie had to ask.

"I've only met her a few times, so I really can't say." Zack pushed the rim of his hat down, hiding his face.

This was getting interesting.

The familiar two-story home with the green shutters came into sight. She imagined Gramps whittling horses on the wrap-around porch. She expected to see Granny running down the steps with a ready hug. The memories forever etched in her heart. The Smith family loved her unconditionally.

Garrett brought her here a little over a week ago. She should be stronger since she'd already had a chance to explore the home, to search the attic, to read from her diary. Still, she ached for her family and what was no more.

She dismounted, tying her horse to a hitching post at the side of the house.

"You okay?" Zack asked, placing his hand on her shoulder.

"Yes," she choked out, not the least bit okay at the moment. Besides missing her family, she wanted a relationship with Garrett. His family was important to him, so a lot rode on this day.

"Good." Zack whistled for Duke and headed along the walkway that led to the back of the house with Kristy following him.

"Hope you're hungry. My dad's grilling steaks." Garrett sexy grin had her falling a deeper under his spell.

Then she thought about his parents. Her body got twitchy inside.

"Come on." Garrett took her hand.

Voices droned as they entered the backyard. Kristy and Zack were several feet ahead. She and Garrett crossed the grass toward a covered patio. He continued holding Josie's hand. Her fingers warm and pleasant. She immediately recognized Mickie, the dark-haired aunt who owned the bakery. Someone familiar in a sea of so many strangers. She let out the breath she didn't know she'd been holding.

"Hey, Garrett, Josie," Mickie waved them over to a picnic table, her smile wide.

"Nice to finally meet you." A man offered his hand to her. "I'm Al. Garrett's favorite uncle."

Hesitantly, she put out her hand, and he shook it. How odd? Only men shook hands in her time.

"You wish," Garrett's softened expression said the two were close.

"Where you from, Josie," Al asked.

"Granite Heights." She cast her focus downward. The last thing she wanted to do right now was talk about herself.

"I hate to cut this short, but I'm starving," Garrett said. "See you guys in a few minutes."

"It is a pleasure meeting you," Josie waved.

Garrett brought her to a table filled with a large assortment of foods. "Here you go," he gave her a paper plate and for the first time in minutes, dropped his hold on her.

"Who's your friend?" a tall and lanky teen turned from the line in front of them.

"What?" another teen pivoted. Both boys identical. From their blond hair to their squared jaws to their short-sleeved shirts in different colors.

"Josie, meet my cousins, Dax and Dawson."

"Is she your girlfriend?" one boy asked.

"Yeah, we're dating." Garrett's lips quirked up at the corners a smidgeon.

Don't overthink the situation. Just relax and get some food. She added potato salad, corn on the cob, rolls, and a slice of watermelon to her plate.

"Lucky dog," the other teen winked.

"What's Mia been up to?" Garrett asked. "She's my cousin," he whispered to her.

"My sister's in love." One twin rolled his eyes upward.

"Yeah. She met some cowboy. Got a glimpse of him at the Fourth of July party, but haven't seen her since." The other teen moved next to a silvery grill with smoke wafting up.

"That must be the guy Tyler has checking out horses in Montana," Garrett said.

"Probably." With his plate full, the closest twin scrunched his brows and moved toward his brother and some other teens crowding around a table underneath a eucalyptus tree.

Garrett stepped behind her to the lit barbecue where a man flipped steaks. "Hey, dad. This is Josie."

Her throat went dry.

His dad's mouth lifted into a grin. "Nice to meet you. Are you the woman Zack hired?"

"Yes, sir."

"Is rare okay with both of you?" his dad asked, setting a large steak on Garrett's plate.

"I'd prefer medium if you have it." Might as well be honest.

His dad added a piece of meat to her dish. "Garrett, can I speak to you for a minute?"

"Sure." He winced which seemed odd to Josie. "Go ahead and have a seat. I'll join you in a minute."

With a plate in her hand, she sat at the picnic table across from Mickie and Al and glanced over at Garrett. His dad spoke with his hands as he glowered at his son. Then Garrett marched over, eased in next to her, his muscular jean-clad thigh pressing against hers.

"Everything okay," Josie asked.

His shoulders stiffened. "Fine." He picked up a knife and started cutting his steak. No, more like sawing it.

She wanted to ask more, but Zack plopped to the right of her. "Hey, everyone."

"Good to see you again." Al held out his hand.

Okay. Now wasn't the right time to sate her curiosity about Garrett's relationship with his dad. Besides, it really was none of her business.

"Mind if we join you?" April moved in by Mickie and pulled her infant son on her lap.

"As if you have to ask?" Mickie said. "May I hold Noah?"

"Please."

Tyler set a plate in front of his wife and sat by her.

"Hey." Tyler eyed Josie. "Heard you're working with Zack."

"I am."

"She's great with horses. A real natural," Zack cut in, which was good because Josie's mouth didn't seem to work.

Kristy strolled up, holding a dirt-streaked little girl. "Charlotte's been having a blast in the sandbox. "Is it alright if I take her into the house to get cleaned up?"

"Be my guest," April said with a laugh. "As much as I love my kids, I'll never turn down a helping hand."

"Do you have any nieces or nephews, Josie?" Mickie asked.

"None." She'd always wondered what it would be like if Dusty kept the ranch. With her brother's over-abundant patience, she figured he'd make a great dad. And she be the aunt who spoiled her nieces and nephews rotten. But that dream had been crushed long ago.

Everyone talked and joked around, reminding her of the fun times she used to have at this very place. Except she wasn't part of this family. Just a visitor that happened to stay next door.

"We're up next in horseshoes," Zack motioned to Garrett, Tyler, and Al.

The men headed for the dirt pit near the back of the fenced-in yard. Again, nostalgia hit her. Behind this house, there used to be miles of open land. Her grandfather didn't believe in unnecessary fences. She imagined him shuttering at this closed-off space.

"I think someone needs to be changed." Mickie handed the baby to April and she scurried off.

"Garrett and Zack are good guys," Mickie said.

"They seem to be, but I've only known them a few weeks." Josie tried to keep her tone steady, keep her voice from hitching. She finished the last bite of steak, threw her plate in the trash, and strolled over to the horseshoe pit.

A sliding glass door from the back of the house opened, and a brunette wearing a floral sundress and a large floppy hat edged in next to her. Her forest green eyes sparkled as she smiled at Josie. "I'm Susan, Garrett's mom. This is my first chance to take a breather."

"Nice to meet you. My name's Josie." She kept her

voice chipper. Had his mom seen her and Garrett holding hands earlier?

"How do you like working with Zack?"

"Very much." Why did people always ask her about Zack? Sure, she'd been working her bottom off, but that had been her choice. She liked being useful and earning her keep. It gave her a sense of pride when she could see the stalls clean or the horse's groomed. But that was her job.

"I've heard you have a knack with horses." Susan's smile appeared genuine.

"My grandfather used to whisper to them. It seems to work." She bit her bottom lip to keep her tears at bay.

Two hours later, their group headed back to Fairfield Farms. Josie had lost count of the names of the family members she met. Everyone had been friendly enough, although trying to keep up with all the names and their conversations had been exhausting.

"You did great." Kristy trotted her horse to her right. "Going in front of that group can be daunting, and I've known them for years. They mean well."

"I-I had fun." The food had been great, the people

friendly, plus she took pleasure beating Garrett at horseshoes. Shadows dappled through the leaves of the trees as they reached the front of the stables.

"How are you holding up?" Zack asked. "I mean visiting a place from your past can't be easy."

"I miss my grandparents." Seeing the farmhouse hit her hard in the stomach, clenching and twisting up old memories that were raw and poignant.

"Try learning your town is underneath a lake." Zack tied his horse to the hitching post. "If I want to visit Cedar City, I need to scuba dive."

"Cedar City is gone?" Zack hadn't mentioned this before.

"They flooded the town in the name of progress." He unbuckled the saddle, lifted it off his horse and went inside the stable.

"I'd better talk to Zack." Kristy rushed behind him.

"Is-is he okay?" Her chest tightened. The last thing she wanted to do was upset her friend.

"He should be." Garrett shrugged.

"It must not seem fair to Zack. I've been fortunate enough to see my family's ranch, while Zack has nothing left of his time."

Garrett had his saddle in his hand. "He can get a bit sentimental."

"Is there anything I can do to support him?"

"Working in the stables is more than enough." When he reached over her arms and unbuckled the cinch, her heart quivered at his gentle touch. His hot breath lingered on her neck. "Helping you makes my day." He carried both saddles.

She followed behind him, ogling his sinewy, muscular arms. And the way his wranglers hugged his derriere, my goodness.

Garrett turned and winked, and her pulse sped faster than the wheels on a stagecoach.

CHAPTER 25

Moonlight cast a soft glow along Garrett's face as Josie sat next to him on a blanket underneath the stars. Several yards below their grassy knoll water lapped along the shore of the Majestic River. Soothing and Constant. Buttercup snorted and grazed on the hillside next to Garrett's mount, Legacy.

Garrett's face appeared shadowed, darkened by the night's sky. "Thought you deserved a little celebration tonight."

"Why?"

"It's August eighth. You've been here a month."

"Already. The days have just flown by." How considerate of him to remember. The more time she spent with him, the more she fell under his spell.

Light reflected off a bottle in his hand. "Thought

we'd celebrate with champagne." He popped the cork and poured the fizzy liquid into two clear plastic cups. "To you, Josie."

"You're too good to me." She clicked her cup with his.

"I do my best." His mouth tipped up with an endearing grin, and she'd swear her heart did a loop-de-loop.

Finished with her drink, bubbles tickled down her throat.

He refilled her cup. "Here's to your first month at the bunkhouse."

"The best month of my life. Especially after meeting you." She drank greedily enjoying the slight fruity taste mingling with effervescent delight.

"Thirsty, huh."

"Can't help myself. This is delicious." She admired his broad chest and wondered what it would be like to run her fingertips against his muscles.

"I almost forgot this." He handed her a bakery bag of snickerdoodles.

His action reminded her of a hero in a romance novel. Ever since she read a Harlequin Romance about a paramedic who resembled Garrett, Josie blushed thinking about the sensual things written in that steamy book. She set her cup down and stuffed a cookie in her mouth and savored the cinnamon delight. "Garrett Kellogg, you are a god."

"I like the way you think." His index finger went under her chin, tipping her up to look directly at him. The simple touch caused fire to heat against her skin.

She sucked in a breath, practically melting by the hot gaze he gave her. Those devastating emerald eyes were doing her in, making her body fevered and tingly inside. He tangled his fingers through her hair and pulled her to him.

"Kiss me," she whispered, needing him to claim her with his mouth.

His arm slipped around her waist, his body rock-solid, strong and hard. Masculine. His firm, full, sexy lips brushed back and forth against hers and their mouths meshed. Tantalizing and naughty urges pushed through her mind as she sank against his chest as he deepened the kiss. His tongue darting with her, tasting like champagne, cinnamon, and sin. He seemed to ignite fire inside her whenever they were together.

A seductive purr hummed over his lips. "The things you do to me." He pulled away leaving her breathless.

"Is that bad?

"It might be." His throaty chuckle shouldn't cause

hot shivers to shoot up her arms and settle in her chest or make her face sizzle when the night air was cool and pleasant.

"Do you miss anything about the past?" He once again refilled their cups, emptying the bottle.

"I miss the open land and the simpler way of life, but I don't miss the inability to make decisions regarding my own future."

"Was your dad really that controlling?"

"Not exactly controlling. Most of the time he pretty much ignored me, which I didn't mind." She downed the rest of her drink. "To be honest, I prefer being here with you."

"I'm glad." He kissed her again. Yearning ratcheted up. Her mind became a symphony of sensations sending her brain into a dizzying spiral of need. Need for him. Need she didn't quite understand.

With his legs outstretched, he brought her onto his lap while he kept on teasing and tasting and driving her mad for him until her lungs were starved for oxygen.

Her hands shifted underneath his shirt and massaged the muscles of his back, roaming his bare skin before tracing her fingernails along his spine.

"Oh, Josie," his voice came out hoarse and raspy. He ripped the shirt over his head.

He unbuttoned her blouse and skimmed his

fingers along her skin until he grasped the lacy edges of her bra. One hand went behind her back and unclasped the garment. His mouth feathered kisses down her neck until he reached her breasts. His tongue flicked against her nipple. The center pebbled hardened, swelling with a swift longing that filled her very essence. He repeated the process on her other breast, alternating the pressure between heavy and light, over and over until she let out a little moan.

"You like that," he whispered.

"Umm," she hummed.

Delightful kisses tickled along her neck, her shoulders, her chin, and her whole body burned with desire. Then he crushed his mouth against hers. His lips were perfect, firm, warm with just the right amount of moisture.

Gently sucking her lower lip, teasing, biting, nibbling and kissing her long and deep. His tongue boldly swept in with hers. Joining in, she melded with him. Opening her jaw wider, she tipped her head back, driven by raw animal need. Sparks hotter than a forest fire shot through her.

And she let out a little sigh. With the way she was losing control, she was in big trouble.

Still sitting on his lap with her bottom against his crotch, she could feel the evidence of his arousal. She wiggled against him. Even though he wore thick denim jeans, she could swear it swelled. She licked her lips. If this was just the taste of what he could offer, she wanted everything. She pushed him back with her on top of him.

"Slow down, babe." He set her to his side, tracing her jaw with his thumb. "You're so beautiful." In the moonlight, she could see his disarmingly seductive eyes studying her, the barest tinge of a smile picking up the corners of his lips.

"So are you," she said softly, and ran her fingertips over him, reveling in his hard-sculpted chest splattered with curly dark hair. Watching him gaze at her with his eyes glazed with passion, she thought him the most attractive man she'd ever seen. She couldn't resist flicking her tongue along his abs.

"You're driving me wild," he moaned. His mouth branded her as his fingertips slid down along her stomach and further down to undo the button on her jeans and unzip them. "I have to see you." He pulled them off. Leaving her bare except for the thong underwear she'd bought with Kristy. His palms slid underneath her buttocks, kneading her, spanning her hips with his hands.

Every touch he gave her made her hot. Blazing hot. Shooting star hot.

And then he trailed kisses down her waist,

pressing his lips against her abdomen, exploring every inch of her, encircling his tongue in her belly button and moving lower. His beard stubble rubbed against her skin, scratchy, abrasive, oh so wicked, making her whimper.

"I have to taste you." He peeled off her panties.

The way Garrett gazed at her heat flared inside her very center.

"Is that okay?" he asked.

Quivering with anticipation, she nodded.

He pushed her legs up and spread them slightly, settling his head between her thighs. His tongue pushed against her womanly folds, licking her, tasting her, teasing her and making her rock against his face. Urging him for more.

"You're perfect," he moaned.

Her fingernails combed restlessly through his hair. Begging for release of some kind, her hips rotated in rhythmic circles. "Oh, Garrett."

"I know babe," he crooned and continued teasing her clit with his tongue. Slipping a finger inside her folds.

She gasped. Surprised at the invasion but not the least bit upset. In fact, she liked what he was doing.

"Are you okay?"

"D-don't stop." She meant it, not exactly sure

what to expect but determined to enjoy every second with him.

He stoked her, in and out, taking her higher and higher, her breath becoming shorter, raspier, while his tongue continued to torment her.

"I need," she moaned.

She was pretty sure he laughed because air tickled her down below, and he slowed his pace, dragging out her desire. All she knew was that the red ember of heat inside was growing into a blaze. He kept toying with her, his finger moving in and out slowly, picking up speed, slowing again, all the while twirling and swirling that wicked tongue against her sensitive spot. Then he added a second finger, the pressure building, demanding something. "Garrett," she gave a hoarse cry. And then she broke, spiraling out of control, her body shuddering as she rode ripple after ripple of pleasure.

Grinning, he moved up next to her and held her in his arms as she came down from the bliss he had given her. Bliss she never knew was possible.

"That was marvelous."

"Yes, you were."

Glancing down at her naked body, she realized he still wore his jeans. "You're not playing fair." Feeling brave, she reached for his belt.

"Hold on, babe. I think it's best if we stop now." His voice came out gruff and insistent.

"Don't you want to make love to me?" There was no telling how long she might remain in his century and she wanted him to initiate her into womanhood.

"Hell, yes. But … you're a virgin. I think you should wait till you're ready."

"I am ready. Please, Garrett. Make love to me." She cupped his face and brought her mouth to his, showing with her kiss what her words had said, branding him, making him pant as much as she was.

They kissed hot and heavy. She dragged her fingernails across his bare chest, continuing lower and this time he allowed her to unbuckle his pants and push down the zipper. Then she slipped her hand inside and squeezed his growing bulge, surprise at how warm and big he was. This brazen act. Totally against her upbringing.

"Are you sure?" he moaned. "The first time might hurt. It can be uncomfortable."

"Will there be more pleasure after the discomfort?"

"Absolutely." He rolled her onto her back, and they kissed until they both were out of breath. "I really should stop."

"Don't stop," she whimpered.

"Fine," he reached into his pocket, pulled out a plastic wrapper.

"What's that?"

"A condom. This will keep you from getting pregnant." He shucked his boxers. She watched in awe. Her hand covered his member, and she couldn't resist giving a little squeeze.

"You're so sexy."

Moonlight glimmered off the intensity in his eyes, his angular face, his serious mouth. A zap of heat hit her as she gazed at his erection, and she found herself squirming, craving for more.

The fact that his hands were trembling as he undid the wrapper and slipped on a condom said he was as anxious as she. He kissed her again, dipping two fingers into her womanly folds.

A ridge of flesh pressed against her stomach. A soft glow from the moon shone on him as he rose above her, gazing into her eyes. The tip of his member pressed against her entrance. His hips rolled slowly, forcing her legs to open wider, inching the tip inside of her, his eyes catching hers. He eased in slowly, his bulge stretching her barrier which stung for the briefest second.

She let out a little, "Eek," as he broke past her barrier. "You're so big and warm."

And he stopped. "Are you all right?"

"Y-yes." She wrapped her legs around his hips as his length filled her completely. Greedy for their closeness. Her pain quickly turned to sensitivity. Awareness of their joining. She dug her fingers into his back clinging to him as the rest of the world started to fade. He moved in and out. Slow and steady. Every sensation making her hotter and happier. His pace picked up, each thrust bringing her closer, heating her from the inside out. Their hearts beat as one, their body attuned to each other. Their passion driving her on.

"Oh, Josie." His growl came out feral.

Desire pounded through her, thrumming through her veins. He brought her to the edge again and again until she whimpered. And once again she spiraled out of control, rippling with such a powerful intensity that she quivered over and over in the most exquisite ecstasy, exploding into a bliss deep and delicious. Her pleasure knocked the air from her very existence. Sending wave after wave of gratification. Like fireworks exploding inside her. Sizzling. Brilliant.

He rammed into her one more time. She heard him call out her name as liquid-warmth her core.

She lay there for the longest time with him holding her. "That was incredible."

He held her in his arms as she slowly stopped trembling. “It sure was.” He pulled her closer.

And at this very moment, there was no doubt in her mind. She was hopelessly in love with Garrett Kellogg.

CHAPTER 26

Garrett spotted Josie in the distance and slowed his strides as he neared the stables. Last night, he'd taken her virginity, and he figured things would be awkward. What does a guy bring a girl after that? He'd considered picking wildflowers, but given the summer heat, most flowers had turned brown. Probably for the best. She might consider the gift an apology for making love with her, and he wasn't the least bit sorry.

He'd promised to take her riding today. And Garrett always tried to keep his promises.

She had her back to him brushing Buttercup's mane. Her curly hair pulled back in a ponytail. The dark red streaks glistened in the sun. She turned, her sweet mouth curving into a grin, and he could swear that ice that had once coated his heart seemed to melt.

Where'd that idea come from? This was ridiculous. Josie was just a woman. A woman who had changed over the last month, smiling more, laughing more, acting like she belonged here. A part of him hoped it was because of him.

He reached into his pocket and pulled a bag he forgotten about.

She peeked inside, suddenly pressing a kiss to his cheek. "You bought me gumdrops." She opened the bag, plopping a sweet morsel into her mouth, making a kittenish purr as she chewed.

Damn. She had no idea how beautiful she was. How her little noises fueled his body. How irresistible he found her. "Let me see." He pulled her against him, leaning down, sampling her mouth, sweeping his tongue inside hers, tasting the sweetness of the candy mixed with a hint of coffee.

She pushed at his chest. "I thought we were going riding."

"We are." Good. She didn't want to talk about last night. Hell, if things went as planned, he'd make love to her again once they reached a secluded cove up in the hills. "You up for a race."

"Always. What are the stakes?" Her eyes flared up like hot blue flames.

"The loser buys lunch." He got on Legacy.

"Get ready to open your wallet." She mounted Buttercup. "Thanks for saddling her for me."

He didn't mind. In fact, he liked helping her, doing things that made her happy. "I was thinking we'd race along the path by the railroad tracks 'till we reach the stone cottage."

"I know the house." Her brows pressed together.

"Is there a problem?"

"Not at all. I was just picturing myself in the lead." Her whole face beamed as she gazed at him.

"Confident, are you?"

"About beating you, of course." She gave him a you're-in-trouble look.

They rode along a dirt path, turned north up Buckshot Road and kept going until they reached the highway. A car honked, and he settled his horse as they waited for a string of vehicles to pass.

"This stretch sure has changed. I think I like it better when the roads were dirt."

"They're functional but lack the connection to nature."

"I think that's why I've always loved the ranch. It's a place where a person can think." She smiled that award winning smile, and damn if his pulse didn't pick up three-fold.

"Come on, the trails on the other side, and I believe you mentioned you'd be buying lunch."

"Not if I win." Since things seemed to be back to normal, winning really didn't matter to him.

She must've learned the roll of her eyes from Kristy. "The cars have cleared. Let's cross." She trotted Buttercup across the pavement and slowed by the train tracks.

"On your mark, get set, go." She kicked her mare.

He took off, glancing sideways at her, noting that she kept a wide girth from the tracks. Leaning forward, her legs gripped Buttercup, her body hovering like a jockey as she followed the horse's gait. Her expression serious and determined.

And holy hell, she was sexy.

A rumbling reverberated behind him.

Vreeeee. A whistle broadcasted an approaching train.

He and Josie kept on riding side by side, not slowing, not looking back.

In the distance, the stone cottage came into view. "I'm winning," she called, looking backward at him.

"For now!" he shouted.

Something shimmered beside him. Something that looked like a transparent locomotive.

"Mercy." Her hand went against her neck, and she lost her balance. Time seemed to slow as he watched her fall off her horse toward a glimmering ribbon of light and disappear along with the phantom train.

"What the heck?" He stared at the riderless horse. Josie had just vanished. Vanished into thin air. Vanished like she'd never been there.

No. No. No.

That didn't just happen. She couldn't be gone. There has to be a reasonable explanation for this.

"Josie!" he shouted. "Where are you?"

Maybe he was seeing things. Rubbing his eyes, he noticed Buttercup cantering without a mount.

"Josie, come back. Don't leave me," he called into the wind. "Please don't let her be gone."

He kept on riding. Maybe begging would work. "If you bring her back, I promise I'll treat her right!" he shouted to whoever might be listening.

Nothing changed.

Catching up to Buttercup, he grabbed the reins, slowing the horses to a stop.

Josie disappeared as if she had slipped through a hole in the atmosphere. His chest heaved in heavy breaths. His muscles were numb.

He'd lost her. One minute she was riding like the wind, pleased with herself because she was in the lead. The next she was gone. Gone like she never existed.

Why had he taken her riding along the tracks?

He'd heard stories about a transparent locomotive that seemed to appear out of nowhere—nicknamed the Ghost Train. He should have connected the locomotive to her arrival. After all she had departed from a train. It felt like someone stabbed a knife in his chest and kept twisting over and over as if toying with his mind.

He shook off the anguish and prayed for her to come back.

"Josie," he called once more.

He had no idea how long he waited on his horse before all hope died. He'd never see her again. Ever.

His chest tightened. His legs were numb. Hell, his muscles were weak, listless. His hand screamed with the pain that shot all the way to his shoulder.

Why did she have to leave now? At the back of his mind, he knew she might return to her time.

Except Zack never did so he'd never seriously considered Josie would go back.

He had to do something. Anything.

Call Zack. He'll understand and maybe have some ideas. He snatched his phone out of his saddlebag. It rang and rang and rang. The sun sat halfway in the sky meaning it would be about noon. Zack should be home.

He couldn't wait here any longer.

Holding Buttercups reins, he kneed his horse to a

trot, would have galloped but handling two horses could be tricky, plus his mind wasn't in the best of shape. The short ride back turned out to be way too many grueling minutes. He rode to the stables in a fog.

Zack looked up from the horse he groomed and waved.

CHAPTER 27

Garrett raced by her side along the railroad tracks, but Josie had the lead. "I'm winning," she shouted.

Something felt off when she heard a locomotive's whistle blast from behind. Her ears prickled from an inner sense she couldn't quite place. Her necklace burned against her throat, and she pulled the locket away with her hand, rubbing the garnet center, losing her balance.

Then she was falling, falling, falling.

The earth seemed to spin like a hyper kaleidoscope of colors. The light too bright. Pain pounded in her temples, and she shut her eyes.

Wheels clacked on a train track. She couldn't be on a train. She was riding Buttercup. Except right now, she was pretty sure she wasn't outside. Wind didn't rush against her face and neck.

Deep down she knew what just happened.

She didn't want to look, but curiosity got the better of her, so she peeled open her eyes slowly … and groaned.

Darn it.

She was indeed inside a passenger compartment, sitting on a plush green bench near the window.

Shaking her head, she blinked. Once, twice, a million times. This had to be an illusion.

She clutched her fist, her nails pushing into her palms. A portly man sat at the bench directly across from her. He set *a* newspaper down next to him.

"May I borrow this?" she asked, pointing to the paper.

"Help yourself."

Picking up the pages, she read the top.

High Desert Weekly Gazette

July 1890

Her throat closed up, tightening like a noose. She couldn't be back on the same locomotive as over a month ago. Dash it all. Her chest squeezed her heart. The beat unevenly.

She fiddled with the stiff collar of her powder-blue blouse. Not the soft T-shirt she had worn moments earlier.

Worry filled her mind.

A sense of desolation permeated in her soul.

Waiting several seconds. Breathing in and out. In and out.

She glanced down at her floor-length skirt. Not jeans. She wanted to be wearing jeans.

Her muscles twitched, and she leaned back into the seat, hoping to find a bit of clarity in this strange situation. Her eyes darted around the area, focusing on the same older man from before sitting across from her. The same group of cowboys laughed from their seats at the front of the passenger car. The young mother in a long dress held the same baby in her lap

"Next stop, Hesperiaaaaaaa," the conductor shouted.

She held onto a last glimmer of hope.

Poking her head out the window, wooden store-fronts lined the main street.

She recognized the dentist office where her grandfather had a tooth extracted.

The bakery with its sweet goods. Her mind drifted to Garrett handing her a bag of snickerdoodles as a surprise.

She held back the sob that wanted to slip out. All she had now were her memories of him, of her new friends, of the bunkhouse that had become her home.

But that life was over. She wanted to be anywhere but 1890 Hesperia.

Forget that. Anywhere but here or in Granite Heights.

"We need to unload lumber and livestock. We'll reboard in two hours.," the porter announced. "Feel free to head over to the hotel. They'll be offering complimentary coffee or lemonade and fresh-baked cookies."

She could wait inside the car—should wait inside the car while she figured things out.

Brakes squealed to a stop right in front of the jailhouse. A man in a black vest had a tin star sparkling in the sunlight. For a second, she thought he might be Garrett. He took off his Stetson and waved to the passengers, flashing dark curly hair. Her heart might as well have seized with the pain that squeezed her chest.

Quit that.

Think about your next step?

Might as well get off while I wait for the departure.

It still baffled her that she wore her 1890 clothing. When she arrived in the future her clothes stayed the same. But in this case, the fact she didn't dress Twenty-first Century items worked in her favor. Acceptable women were not seen in public wearing trousers.

She adjusted her wide-brimmed hat, held her bag in one hand, her pocketbook in the other and moved up the aisle behind a woman carrying a baby and reached the top of the metal-grated steps. On the walkway next to the train, women strolled along in floor-length dresses, men in suits or jeans and cotton shirts with vests.

No sense denying, she was back in nineteenth century.

She would scream, cry, throw a tantrum if it would do any good. But she knew better. What she needed to do was act calm and rational. Come up with a plan.

She still had silver dollars sewn into her hem of her petticoat. She could afford a room at the Hesperia Hotel.

Although, she could care less where she went. All she wanted to do was to go back to the bunkhouse.

As she looked down from the top of the car, she spotted the livery. They rented horses. Why not rent one for herself and ride out toward the farmhouse?

CHAPTER 28

Garrett arrived home at two a.m. from a crazy, busy shift and headed for his room. He'd been thankful for the constant calls because when it got quiet, his mind wandered. Wandered to the fact Josie was gone and would most likely never be back. And that thought kept gnawing at his gut.

It didn't help that love songs played on the radio during his drive back to the farm. Not that he had been in love with her.

No. Not him.

He liked giving her gifts that made her smile. He liked spending time with her. He liked kissing her. But that wasn't love.

Besides, she came from wealth. She belonged with a rich man, not a broken catcher like himself who never even made it to the majors. She deserved fancy dresses and expensive jewelry and a big house.

He scrubbed his hands over his face, frustration building inside him. "Why the hell do I miss her so much?"

He stripped down to a pair of boxers and got under the covers. What he needed right now was rest. Despite everything, he blamed himself. If he hadn't brought her to the train tracks, she would be asleep in the room right next to his. Maybe sleeping beside him.

So, he opened the door to her room. The space felt vacant. Deserted without Josie there.

The door squeaked. He ambled by the massive dresser. Pencils and charcoal neatly lined a tray next to her sketchbook. He picked it up, sat on the edge of the twin bed, and flipped through the pages. There were countless drawings of Buttercup, drawings of Zack and Kristy, and far too many drawings of him. One showed her and him sitting close on a blanket, their lips inches apart.

This was too much.

His chest tightened, squeezing away the part of him that hoped for happiness. He knew better than to give into this illusion. After all, his life had been filled with plenty of disappointments.

Get over yourself. You never deserved her

anyway. Whatever you had with her was temporary from the get-go.

He set the drawings back where they belonged. His gaze drifted to a brown leather book on the end table. Her diary. He flipped through the pages.

One morning my mom went riding. Her horse came back without her.

Hmm … was this a coincidence? Maybe. Maybe not.

He leaned back on the bed, holding the diary against his chest, breathing in the rose scent on her pillow. He recalled visiting the attic with her. Her eyes had lit with excitement when she held up her grandmother's comforter. He promised to bring the chest to her room but never got around to it.

No time like the present.

GARRETT LUGGED the chest up to his room. Downstairs, the grandfather clock chimed four times. Adrenaline charged through his system, making him wide awake. He sat on the edge of his bed and lifted out the old patchwork quilt.

Something thudded on the floor.

He picked up a stack of envelopes tied with a

blue satin ribbon with *Garrett* carefully inscribed on the front with a delicate, embellished penmanship.

"What the heck?"

Untying the bow, his hands were clammy as he opened the wax seal.

July 11, 1890

Dear Garrett,

I don't know if you will ever read this, but I hope you do. I'm sure you were as shocked to see me gone as I am devastated to have ended up back in 1890. It's not fair. I finally find a place where I felt like I truly belonged only to have everything snatched away in a split second.

Right now, I don't want to be here. I've been staying at the abandoned farmhouse for the past four days. I needed to take a few weeks to regather my bearing. Soon my father will be looking for me, and I'll have to go ahead with the arranged marriage.

I'm not ready to head for Granite Heights and am determined to find a way back to you. My hopes and dreams in this era are limited. Women have more opportunities in the future. Since I disappeared along the railroad tracks, I'm assuming I'll return the same way. Nine times now, I have attempted to recreate the scene, racing along the tracks until I reach the stone cottage.

Tomorrow, I will make it work. I will see you again. I must see you again.

I miss you, Garrett. So much. This place is empty without you. It's funny. I can almost see you reading my words. Smiling at me like you did when I refused to let you carry my saddle. Telling me, "You go, girl," and making me giggle.

The farmhouse is vacant except for a couple of mice. I'm completely alone for the first time in my life. I've always lived with family and servants or at the bunkhouse with my new friends. I've been cooking basic meals like biscuits and bacon. Whenever I walk into the kitchen, I expect to see a large white refrigerator filled with delicious food. I expect to grab a burrito out of the freezer compartment and throw it in the microwave. How I miss the future.

I've been gathering hay for my rented horse, Rascal, who had become my only friend here. He's good-natured and sometimes answers me with a nod of his head, a whinny, or when I say something ridiculous, he snorts.

If I could make it back, I'd like to be an artist or maybe even a horse whisperer. Dreams that I seriously doubt could ever happen in my time.

Today, while rifling through my grandfather's rolltop desk, I found his old ledgers and thought about him sitting at this very chair to do the task. Then I discovered a fountain pen, ink, paper, and several envelopes. So here I am, missing you something fierce and writing down my thoughts.

Love,

Josie

JULY ELEVENTH? It's now August, Garrett thought. Wait. Josie arrived on July eighth in his time, and today it's August thirteenth. Okay, this doesn't quite make sense. Neither did the fact she'd written him a letter in the nineteenth century.

He had to admire how she thought things through by coming back to the farmhouse determined to get back to the future. She sounded upbeat. Forever an animal lover, she befriended her horse when there was nobody else to talk to. He could almost see Josie, sitting at the desk, her shoulders squared, eyes focused on the page as she wrote to him.

HE OPENED THE NEXT LETTER.

JULY 14, 1890

Dear Garrett,

I've been here for a week now. In-between my trips to

the train tracks, I try to keep busy. My few outfits are getting worn. When I went up to the attic and found some men's clothes, I must have screamed so loud my voice could be heard for miles. I've had to make adjustments, using rope for a belt to tighten up the waist and rolling up the bottoms. There are half a dozen flannel shirts. I've used them when I'm out riding.

A little later, I plan to heat water on the stove and revel in a cast iron bathtub in the room off from the kitchen. This will be my first attempt. Mercy, I miss the feel of a hot shower. I've bathed at the river, but the murky water never gets me clean enough.

Whenever I am near the river, I find myself stopping at our special spot. The tree is half the size it was when we picnicked underneath. That night under the stars keeps me striving to return to you.

On that note, I shall bid my farewell.

Love,

Josie

She'd been so beautiful that night with her long red hair flowing freely, her mouth teasing and tempting him. With his resistance gone, he took her virginity underneath the moonlit night.

He shook his head. *Stop it. I'm not the sentimental type.* Except with Josie, he found himself thinking about her, wanting her, yearning for what would never be. He picked up another letter.

July 18, 1890

Dear Garrett,

Ten days have gone by. Lately, I've had some insightful conversations with my horse, Rascal. Ha! Well, he's more of a listener. Kind of like you. No offense, but I just compared you to a horse. Although you should take it as a compliment. Horses are intelligent, majestic creatures.

Now I'm just getting loopy.

I should scratch out the last few sentences. Nope. They make me laugh.

I haven't had much to laugh about lately. It's lonely out here. At night, the wind howls. The shutters rattle. Coyotes yowl for their mates, and all I can think about is getting back to the future and you.

What I am trying to say is that my short time at the bunkhouse taught me much more than you'll ever know. It forced me to grow up. To think for myself. To quit looking over my shoulder in public and pretend to be someone foreign to my nature. To act like the perfect daughter because that was what my father expected of me. All the while knowing I could never be that person deep down inside.

At Fairfield Farms, I was no longer just a rich man's daughter the servants had to wait on. I was true to myself.

It feels good to express my ideas out into the open.

Love,

Josie

HE ALMOST FELT like she was in the room with him talking about her day. Ten days must seem like an eternity. Damn, he wished he could do something to get her back. The chances of her returning were slim, still he couldn't quite let her go.

The grandfather clock chimes six times. Since he had to work tonight, he'd better get some sleep.

Tomorrow, he'd tackled the rest of the letters.

CHAPTER 29

All through his shift, Garrett's mind kept wandering. Josie's in her world, and he missed her.

This wasn't fair. They should have had more time.

He had to accept she'd gone back to where she belonged. Except … he wanted her with him.

Now in his bedroom, he undid the wax seal and opened the next letter.

July 21, 1890

My Dear Garrett,

Two weeks have passed without even a glimmer of the future. Fourteen long days. I've been trying to keep my spirits up, but as each day goes by my hopes and dreams of a better life dwindle and fade away like the last light of a sunset. I miss so much about my short month with you.

I opted to forgo the expense of coffee and didn't think I'd miss drinking it, but I do. I miss how Zack would greet me in the morning with a ready smile and a steaming cup of Joe. I miss Kristy and her constant smile.

But most of all, I miss you, Garrett.

It's time to face my future. Soon, I must head for Granite Heights.

Josie

"I MISS YOU, TOO," he said out loud and picked up the final letter.

JULY 29, 1890

My Dearest Garrett,

This will be my last letter to you. I tried to return to the future, truly I did, giving my all each and every day. This morning I raced along the train tracks as far as the stone cottage and begged for the entrance to open. As before, nothing happened.

At this point after three weeks here, I just ate the last of my food. I have no money to buy more supplies. I refused to cry at what might have been. I must accept my fate and return home.

I have weighed my options carefully and conclude marrying William on August eighteenth seems to be the only feasible choice. He is a respected man and will be a good provider. Once wed, I will honor my vows and do my best to be a suitable wife.

I will never regret a moment I spent with you. I am grateful our paths have crossed. I will always cherish my memories of you. You are kind and giving and the best man I have ever met. I wish you happiness and hope you find the love of your life. Know that you will always hold a special place in my heart. I will never forget you.

Love you forever,

Josie

SHIT. She was saying goodbye. He'd never see her again.

Of course, he knew that, but reading her letters made him feel like she had been in the room with him. Like she wasn't gone. Like there might be hope.

Except in this letter, she'd given up. Not that she had any other choice, but he hated knowing that she'd be forced to marry.

She said goodbye. And there wasn't a damn thing he could do about it.

It's for the best.

Too bad he'd never see her again. Too bad he'd

never get another chance to make love with her. Once hadn't been enough. She'd come into his life like a whirlwind, lassoing him right in, and he wanted more.

It's time to let her go.

Footsteps sounded in the hallway. Zack was up. Might as well talk this out with his friend. He pulled on a T-shirt and jeans and tromped down the stairs. "Morning," He took the barstool where he usually sat and stared at the coffee pot. He needed to ride, to feel the fresh air in his face, to force this angst inside to go away.

"You're up early." Zack set two slices of bread into the toaster and poured liquid in two cups, placing one in front of Garrett. "Need to talk?"

His friend knew him better than anyone, knew his moods, knew when to just wait for an answer. Garrett sipped his coffee, letting the warmth soothe him as the caffeine kicked in. "How'd you guess?"

"First of all, you're never awake this early." Zack shrugged. "What's up?"

"I can't get Josie out of my mind. It's been two days, and I'm wound tighter than a stripped screw. I'm burning inside trying to figure out a possible loophole we haven't thought about."

"You've gotta let her go."

"Don't I know it, but …" He took a big gulp and

the coffee burned down his throat. "I found some letters that she wrote."

"You mean she wrote to you while she stayed in the bunkhouse."

"Not exactly. I found them in an old trunk in the farmhouse attic."

He lifted a brow. "What made you go up in the attic?"

"I went up there with Josie one day and we found her diary in a chest. And when I got home yesterday, I had this intuition to bring the chest back to my room." Which wasn't like him at all. He'd always put intuition on par with tarot cards and hocus pocus.

"The letters seem like some kind of a sign." Zack got up and buttered the toast and handed him a piece.

"It does, doesn't it? I feel like I need to rescue her, but I have no idea if that's even possible. What do you remember about your trip here?"

"Just that one minute I was on a train heading for Hesperia, and the next minute I got off in the future."

"You ended up in Whiskeyville just like Josie, right?"

"Yep."

"Come on, Zack, think. There has to be more to it." Garrett pounded his fist on the counter.

"Your uncle once talked with me about black holes and stuff. Maybe he has an idea."

"You're a genius," Garrett said. "Since Uncle Al's a professor, he should be able to help us. If not, I'm sure he will know someone who can."

"I'm gonna text Uncle Al and see if he can come over later." Picking up his phone, he texted.

I need your help. Call ASAP.

At quarter to eleven, Garrett, Zack and Uncle Al sat in the living room.

"What I'm about to tell you will sound crazy." Garrett tapped his foot, hoping for the right words to spill. "But you're the only one I can think of to help us."

"Okay." Al lifted a brow.

"You remember Josie, right?" He heaved a big breath, leaning his elbow on the armrest.

"Nice girl. You still dating her?"

"I would be but … she slipped back to 1890."

"Are you saying she's a time traveler?

Focusing on his uncle's face, Garrett expected his jaw to drop or his eyes to widen, but Al remained calm and composed without even a flicker or flinch.

"Yes. We were racing along the train tracks, and

she disappeared right in front of my eyes." One minute she's challenging him, her braids flying back, her horse galloping. The next thing she was gone. Poof! Just like a hard punch in the gut.

"What else do you remember?" Uncle Al rubbed his chin.

Hmm … something had happened. What was it? He closed his eyes, trying to recall that moment. The horse's hoofs pounded on the ground. The air whooshed by. "I heard a train whistle several seconds before she vanished."

"Did you see the train?" A brow lifted as Al sat forward.

"Pistons pumped, wheels clacked, and I saw a glimmering translucent locomotive. I'm guessing it was the ghost train."

"I haven't heard that term in ages. Since I never witnessed it myself, all of us brothers, including your dad thought it was a hoax, but your grandfather swore the ghost train existed."

"Believe me, something happened." Garrett wished he could piece all this together.

"There's some kind of connection here." Zack squinted just like he always did when he was thinking.

"Probably. Do you recall what time Josie vanished?"

"I think about three or four."

"I notice the grandfather clock chimes at four when I finish up for the day." Zack rubbed his neck. "One time I'd been right near the tracks. I heard the faint whistle blast. Thought I saw something flickering. I blinked, then it was gone."

"We can assume you were riding around four when the event occurred. Do you have anything else that might help?" Uncle Al put his feet up on the ottoman.

"Josie left me letters. I found them when I brought her trunk from the farmhouse attic."

"May I read them?" his uncle asked.

"Start with the last one. She stayed at the Silver Spur all alone for three weeks determined she'd find her way back to us. Eventually, she resigned to the idea she wasn't coming back." He fought the angst crawling up his throat. "We have to figure out a way to get to her."

"I doubt this will be possible." His uncle scanned the paper.

"You're not the first relative to ask for my assistance with time travel." Al leaned his hands on his knees.

"Who else?" This was getting interesting. His uncle never failed to surprise him.

"Mia. She went back to 1890." Al got up and grabbed a soda from the fridge.

"Wait." Had he heard right? "My cousin's a time traveler?"

"She sure is. She tried to save Dusty Mann from hanging. Here's the kicker. He ended up coming forward in time."

"Could Dusty be Josie's brother?" Zack said. "She never said his name."

"You're right." Garrett wondered if she hadn't mentioned her brother's name because it was too painful to know he was long gone.

"Wouldn't that be a kick?" Al popped his soda and took a sip.

"If it's true, it's kinda sad. Josie went back to the past without never meeting up with her brother." Zack folded his hands. "Wanna hear something ever crazier?"

"Sure." Al raised a brow.

"I'm from Cedar Springs in 1887." Zack folded his hands together. The only ones who knew Zack's secret had been his aunt, uncle, Kristy, and Garrett. This must be hard for him.

"That's amazing. And you've never returned?" his uncle asked.

"Nope."

"If all these people have time traveled, maybe we

could get Josie back." There might be hope for her after all.

Al sipped his drink. "I think we should invite Mia and Dusty over. They can help brainstorm, plus I think they might have a couple of things that could help us." He got out his phone and texted her.

A few seconds later, Al's phone pinged. "She and Dusty are on their way." He picked up his phone and called Mia, filling her in on the whole situation.

CHAPTER 30

Garrett's cousin Mia walked into the bunkhouse clutching the arm of a tall, muscular cowboy. His eyes reminded him of Josie's, except they were gray instead of turquoise. "This is Dusty, my fiancé," Mia's face practically glowed.

"Congrats," Garrett held out his hand to Dusty. Then he gave Mia a hug.

"Let's all sit in the living room. Can I get you coffee, a soda, iced tea?" Zack asked.

"Coffee for both of us, please," Dusty said.

Al placed his hand on Mia's shoulder. "How are you doing?"

"Happier than ever." She kissed Dusty's cheek giving him a dreamy gaze, and the two of them sat at the couch.

Al moved to the left of Mia. "There's a lot to

discuss. It's still hard to believe that the three of you time traveled." He motioned to Mia, Zack, and Dusty.

"As you probably know, Mia saved my neck, literally." Dusty removed his Stetson, his dark russet the same color as Josie's.

"Is Josie your sister?" Garrett asked.

"I have a sister with that name. Why do you ask?" Dusty stared at Garrett.

"After seeing you, there's no doubt you two are related," Zack said.

"You've met my sister?" Dusty's mouth gaped open. "Where is she?"

Garrett felt for the guy. A couple of days earlier, he could have reunited with her.

"We thought Mia might help us figure out how to bring her back, and now that you're here, Dusty, it's an added bonus." Al tented his fingers.

"I'll do whatever I can."

"I was hoping you'd say that." Garrett liked that Dusty didn't waste words.

Al reviewed what they already knew explaining how Josie seemed to disappear right after a ghost train sounded, talked about the letters Josie wrote to Garrett and handed Dusty the final letter to read.

Dusty cocked his head. "Are you and my sister together?"

"We were dating." Garrett's mouth got dry, finding it a little awkward facing Josie's brother since he'd slept with her.

"I see." Dusty's face appeared solemn. "I wish I had known she was here. I haven't seen her in a few years."

"That's why we invited you two over. We're wondering if there is a way to get to her. Maybe bring her back." Al gave a wane smile.

Garrett sucked in a deep breath. If only things could be easy.

"We're not even sure how to open the portal." Al looked at Mia. "You tried, remember?"

"I only tried once. Luckily, Dusty found his way forward to me the next day." Mia squeezed his hand.

"Al, do you have any idea how to open up a portal?" Dusty asked.

"I have my theories. Are you familiar with the Hawking's Projection Conjecture?"

"Not at all." Ask Garrett about baseball rules, plays, or the different speeds with pitches, and he could run circles around most people, but he'd never taken any physics courses.

"Space and time are not static. With the right push, time itself could be altered to jump both forward and backward." Al paused for several seconds, allowing everyone to process the words.

"The push must've happened to Josie and the others," Garrett said.

"Probably. We believe space curvatures fold in on itself." Al picked up a napkin and folded it in half on the coffee table. "Where the two pieces come together, where they touch, they can be bridged."

"There has to be more to this otherwise lots of people would be jumping through time like I did," Dusty added.

Garrett snatched the letter from the table. "Josie's wedding is scheduled for August eighteenth which means even if we figure out a way to her time, she'll already be married."

"That's not true. I landed in the past a month earlier than my departure date." Mia got out her phone and appeared to be counting. "Since today is September second, you should have at least six days to attempt to get her."

"Good to know." Garrett let out a long breath.

Mia folded her arms. "Zack, do you remember how you came to this time?"

"I boarded a train at the summit, heading for Hesperia and ended up getting off in this century." He shook his head. "It's crazy to think Mia, Dusty, Josie and I have time traveled."

"More like mind-boggling." Al shook his head. "This area must have a substantial vortex connection. Although, Mia and I have this theory that the garnet on her ring might be a conductor. We think the same thing may have occurred with the stone on Dusty's belt buckle. Did you bring the items with you?"

"I did." Mia pulled out a plastic bag from her purse and passed it to Al. "Not about to take any chances of opening up another wormhole, I locked the jewelry in the trunk on our way here."

Garrett whistled, noting the quarter-sized stone on the buckle. "Is that a ruby?"

"Garnet," Al said. "Garnets are said to have mystical properties."

"Were you wearing any jewelry when you came here, Zack?" Al asked as he examined Dusty's belt buckle.

"My pocket watch has red stones on the front of the case. I'm pretty sure they're the same color as the belt." Zack raked his fingers through his hair. "My watch belonged to my great-great-grandfather. He'd been out in a storm when a lightning bolt hit a stone and cracked it in two. His wife embedded pieces of that stone into the case for good luck and made other jewelry with the rest. I wonder if these stones are connected."

"Josie's locket had a red stone in it." Garrett had noticed the necklace when he kissed her neck.

Dusty rubbed his jaw. "Originally, I found the belt buckle and Josie's locket in the attic of the Silver Spur farmhouse."

"Sounds like there's a definite connection between the two." The direction this conversation headed might just work.

"Definitely. Mia and Dusty both said their stones got really hot right before they went through the portal. Did that happen to you, Zack?" Al asked.

"Come to think of it, the stones burned against my thigh. Then the room started to spin."

"The string theory must've occurred, causing the dimension to shift." Al picked up a menu from the coffee table. "Think of a model of a DNA, but instead of our bodies, superstrings are larger, more complicated structures that deal with the forces of the universe. Twist them one way, and the strings become a proton—a different way, they become electrons or photons of light or gravitons. The mysterious particles of force create dimensions of space, time or undiscovered energies with up flow and inflow patterns of electrical pulses."

Garrett tried to follow his uncle's train of logic, but shit, this was some heavy stuff. "What do we do to help Josie?"

"Make a plan and hope it works. Since we don't want to gamble with Dusty hanging, I think Zack should be the one to go." Al steepled his fingers. "Are you okay with that, Zack?"

Not once did his uncle consider sending Garrett. Not for a second. And that stung.

"Absolutely. If I do find Josie and we can't make our way through a portal, I can always bring her to Cedar Springs with my family. She'll be safe." Zack could break the wildest horse. Zack could run a farm and work a second job. Zack always had the highest score in miniature golf and bowling. Zack would get the job done.

Of course, this made sense. But Garrett wanted to be the one she looked at with admiration in her eyes when he rescued her. He clenched his right hand and pain shot up his arm. Damn that baseball injury.

"It's almost two. Since the ghost train sounded yesterday at around four, I doubt it will come today, but with only six days before Josie's wedding we should give it a try," Garrett said, feeling the urgency.

"I agree." Al stood. "I'll go home to grab my collection of old coins."

"I'd better draw you a map of train and land routes to Granite Heights, along with a map of where the church is located," Dusty said.

"I'm gonna see if I can find the train schedules

heading north for Granite Heights in 1890. I think I can tap into a museum or university archive." Mia got out her iPad.

"Good idea." Garrett gave a silent plea for success.

CHAPTER 31

Josie removed her straw hat and wiped the perspiration dripping from her forehead as the sun's burning rays beat down on her. Sweat coated her back, between her breast, her sides, even her undergarments. Typical unforgiving desert.

Passing a two-story house with white pillars and a covered porch, she recognized Missy's Boarding House, stopped, and tied her horse to the hitching post. A gray-haired woman in a drab brown dress covered with a white smock stepped onto the veranda. "May I help you?"

"Yes, please." Josie straightened her skirt and walked up the steps. "Are you in need of a housekeeper?" She kept her tone steady.

"I'm sorry, miss." The woman shook her head. "You might try the Hesperia Hotel."

"Thank you for your time." Josie wanted to ask the woman to give her a place to stay. She wanted to beg for a slice of bread or any other leftover food. But she didn't. Instead, she put her foot back in the stirrup and made her way down the dirt road to the stables.

"Howdy, miss," the owner called, taking the reins from her. The short, stocky man wore a friendly grin. The kind of grin that should put her at ease. "Did you enjoy your stay?"

Enjoy. Not exactly the word she'd use to describe the last three weeks. Her time had been filled with hope and plenty of disappointment.

"Are you returning your horse a week early, or did you plan to use your mount for more days?"

"I'm done." She hadn't even made it a full month before she ran out of food.

"You've got a refund coming." He untied her bag from the saddle, headed into the office and came back with four silver dollars.

"Thank you." She had money. Enough money for a meal and train fare back home. "Can you tell me what time the locomotive will arrive today?

"I believe it left about an hour ago."

Her aching stomach rumbled. Scurrying by the blacksmith's shop, a hammer clanged against an anvil. Each pound like an ominous tick as if saying her independence would soon be lost. She trudged along the planked walkways leading to the three-story building, but she had no intention of eating there. Not with their exorbitant prices.

Instead, she kept her head down and rushed toward the bakery, the yeasty aroma luring her inside. The boxy room had scattered tables facing the windows. Counters displayed loaves of wrapped bread. Cookies and cakes were set inside a glass display. She sat at the only empty table which happened to look out at the street.

"Coffee," a woman in a long black dress covered with a floral apron asked.

"Please."

"Our special today is scrambled eggs with country potatoes and Johnny cakes."

"That sounds delicious." She leaned back in her chair, letting out the breath she hadn't realized she'd been holding, and picked up a Hesperia Gazette left on the table. Hmmm … Whiskeyville's Founder's Day Celebration would kick off with a parade. She thought about Founder's Day in the future where she met Garrett. He'd been so handsome in his sheriff's uniform.

Dash it all.

Would she ever stop missing him?

Turning the page, Farmer Joe advertised his fresh fruit and vegetable stand.

The waitress set a plate in front of her. Josie put the paper aside. Taking a bite of eggs, her taste buds practically sang, and she kept on eating. Every morsel better than the last. The potatoes were salty and filling. Adding maple syrup to the stack of pancakes, she decided right then and there she had died and gone to heaven.

"Hello, Josephine," her father said standing in front of her table.

She froze, feeling like a mouse with its tail caught under a cat's claw. Ready to run but too afraid to move, her lungs starved for breath.

He eased into the seat across from here. "You've been gone three weeks. Your little game is over," her father said in hushed tones only she could hear.

"Game?" she fluttered her lashes, something that used to work when she was maybe five. Not her smartest action but mercy, she hadn't expected to be ambushed by him.

"I found a letter from your brother on your desk and hired someone to track you. Knowing how much you adored Dusty, I had a feeling you'd visit him in Hesperia," he said between clenched teeth.

For some unknown reason, her father never cared for her cowboy half-brother. When his mom remarried, Dusty chose to live with his grandparents at the Silver Spur rather than stay in Granite Heights.

"Why didn't you tell me he almost hanged?"

He patted her hand like she were a child. "I didn't want to see you upset."

She could have been at Dusty's trial supporting him instead of being kept in the dark. "You should have told me."

"While you failed to inform me where you were going. Your disappearance scared me."

"Why?" He'd never paid much attention to her before.

"I thought I might never see you again," he paused, his brows snapped together, and his mouth twisted down. Something he never did. Her father usually acted calm and collected, playing his life like a poker game—forever unreadable. But at this moment, she could tell he was dismayed.

"Were you thinking about mom?"

"Yes. That was a dark time." He rubbed his jaw and avoided direct contact with her.

Who knew her father had a heart? "You never said a word about mom, never shed a tear, just shut me out of your life."

"I made sure you were always taken care of."

"If you think that providing a roof over my head,

making sure the servants looked after me and giving me an allowance was enough, you were wrong. I was hurting. I missed my mom, and you didn't seem to care."

"I handled things the best way I could. That's why I arranged your marriage to William. Your future will be secure." He smiled at her, something he never did. "You had your fun. Now it's time to come home."

Just like that, his aloofness was back. Obviously, he preferred being distant rather than have a real conversation with her. He had to be in control. He didn't care about her opinion. Whatever he said was the law of the house.

"I d-don't want to marry William."

"You *do not* have any choice. William doesn't care about a dowry. He's the wealthiest man in Riverside County, and he wants you for his bride. Just think of the prestige you'll have with William as your husband." His dad's posture stiffened, his neck corded, he held his chin high.

"What's in it for you, father?" After many of his expensive horses had been sold, she knew his financial state was declining.

"I get to see my daughter happy."

She wanted to tell him how she had been happier living in the bunkhouse than she ever had been in

Granite Heights, but the point was moot. She didn't have any other options left. She had three weeks until her wedding.

Blessed saints, she didn't like the idea of her future.

"Since you're done eating, we'll go back to the hotel, get you a bath and a decent dress. One that doesn't make you look like you were cleaning out stalls in the stables."

She kept her mouth shut, deciding to choose her own battles.

CHAPTER 32

Garrett got off his horse and waited next to his uncle, Mia and Dusty, while Zack remained astride his mount.

"I almost forgot to give you this. It's all the change I have from the 1800s. There's about forty-five dollars." Al handed Zack a pull-string pouch filled with coins and he tucked the money in his pants pocket. "You ready?"

"Yep." In Levis, a long-sleeved checkered shirt, and a leather vest Zack looked every bit a wild west man. He gave a lopsided grin, rubbed the large garnet on the borrowed belt buckle, and fingered the chain around his neck holding Mia's ring.

Garrett pulled out his phone from his pocket. "If luck's on our side the ghost train will sound in five minutes."

"You have the maps?" Dusty asked.

"Right here with the train schedules." Zack tapped his vest, appearing as cool as ice. "Is this where you started with Josie?" He inched closer to the tracks.

"Sure is." He and Josie walked their horses side by side until she took off. "She disappeared right before the stone cottage."

"Got it."

The sun beat down on them as they waited five minutes, ten minutes, twenty-five minutes. No sound of a whistle blasting. No sign of a phantom locomotive. Not even a flicker of light.

"We knew today was a long shot," his uncle said as he took off his hat and wiped away sweat from his forehead.

Garrett remained rooted in his spot.

"We have to keep trying." Dusty's determined expression reminded Garrett of Josie when she tried to master cooking an omelet on the electric stove. God, he missed her.

"I'm not giving up." Zack turned his horse while Garrett and the others mounted. "I'll come out here every day until I find a way through the portal."

"I need to clear my head." Garrett clicked his horse to a canter heading toward the river. He needed to deal with his frustration alone.

TWO DAYS EARLIER, Garrett and Zack had headed for the railroad tracks. As they crossed the street, they heard the shrill whistle, meaning they had misjudged the time the ghost train should arrive.

Zack immediately took off, yelling, "Yah," galloping to catch up to the shimmering translucent train as it chug-chugged along. He didn't stop until he'd made it about a mile past the stone cottage. But he had been seconds too late.

Today, Garrett hoped the results would be different. Countless times since they'd hatched this plan, he'd begged to whoever was in charge of the portal to open it up. This was their last shot. If they didn't make it back to Josie, she'd be married.

"Hey." Zack waved at him from an outdoor stall.

"You got a minute."

"Yep. I just fed all the horses and thought I'd wash up before we head for the tracks. Is something wrong?"

Besides the fact he had no control over Josie's disappearance. Besides the fact that he missed her so much he could hardly breathe—everything was just peachy. "I have an idea for today."

"Okay." Zack quirked a brow.

"I've got this hunch you should try Buttercup since that's the horse Josie had been riding?"

"That's a good point, but I think we should attempt something else."

"Sure." Garrett would try just about anything. "What is it?"

"You love Josie, don't you?"

"Hell, yes." Surprised he'd admitted that out loud, he glanced at his friend.

"Then go get her."

"Hmm." Zack had been chosen to rescue her for a good reason. Old doubts raised an ugly head as Garrett's father's words resonated in his mind. *You'll never be good enough if you don't give it your all.*

"I know that look. You think you can't do it, but that's a bunch of bull. If anyone should go, it should be you."

Determination threaded through Garrett's mind. "You're absolutely right." *I can do this. I have to do this for Josie.*

"Then let's go." Zack handed over his belt, vest, and pouch with change. "With you going after her, I know it will work this time. She's your destiny."

"Look at you being all philosophical."

"That's me." Zack gave him a goofy grin.

The two of them got on their mounts. At precisely 4:01, Garrett took off along the railroad tracks. "I'm coming Josie." His words tumbled out as the horse's hoofs hit the ground.

A chugging sound came from behind him. The borrowed belt-buckle heated, burning through the layers of clothing. His instinct said to take it off but Dusty told him to rub the stone. Holding both reins in his left hand, Garrett used his fingers and the palm of his right hand to stroke the garnet.

A whistle blared. A rainbow of light twirled in front of his eyes spinning faster than a pinwheel in a hurricane. Some outside force pulled him off the saddle, and he fell toward shimmering light. Dizzy, he closed his eyes.

No wind blew against his face. The back of his seat had become soft and cushiony. Wheels clacked underneath this compartment.

"Next stop, Hesperia," the conductor called.

He peeled open his eyes, staring at an older cowboy facing him on a plush green bench. Smoke puffed from his pipe, filling the room with an acrid smell.

Exhilaration pumped through his veins.

He made it to the past. He really did it.

The train slowed to a stop. A man in a dark suit and derby hat moved up the aisle.

"What's our next stop after this?" the cowboy asked the conductor.

"Whiskeyville."

"Think we'll make it to Daggett by one?"

"Don't see why not." The conductor looked at Garrett and tipped the small bill on his round hat.

Oh, shit. This train's headed northbound while he needed to be going south. Garrett better get off now. Standing and adjusting the backpack on his shoulders, he followed the others down the grated metal steps, onto the platform and kept walking.

He asked a guy in the ticket booth. "What time will the train for Granite Heights depart?"

"Not till Monday at noon."

Dammit. He sucked in a deep breath. "What's today's date?"

"Friday, August seventeenth."

Dusty had mentioned most weddings in his era were performed around two. This meant he had less than twenty-four hours to get to Josie. "Any idea how I can make it there by tomorrow?"

"You could always rent a horse from the livery."

"Good idea." Having to squeeze past an elderly woman on the left, he rushed down a dozen sets of stairs, reached the dirt road and sprinted. His legs and arms pumped, pushing him on until he spotted the tall wooden structure with livery painted in large black letters on the roof. A couple of men took off in a horse and buggy and waved as they passed him.

Garrett entered the building through the open double doors. "Hello," he called into a fairly empty room. Harnesses, reins, and other equipment took up an entire wall. Dozens of stalls filled the left side.

"Over here," a voiced boomed from underneath of a green wagon.

Garrett stepped over and spotted a dark-haired guy hammering a wooden wheel in place.

"May I help you?" The guy got up and gave him a gap-toothed grin.

"I'd like to rent a horse." He hoped it would be less than the forty-five dollars he had in his pocket.

"Can't help you. Just rented out the last one."

Great. Now what should he do? "I need to get to Riverside by tomorrow afternoon. Do you have any suggestions?"

Boots clomped inside. Garrett looked up to a sizeble, stocky guy in overalls. "I can take you as far as San Bernardino tomorrow if you're willing to help me load this wagon with hay at my farm."

A hay wagon would be bulky and slow, but what other choice did he have? "You've got yourself a deal." Garrett shook the guy's massive hand.

CHAPTER 33

Garrett's butt slammed into a hard-wooden seat. Never again would he take his truck's cushioned bench for granted. Even worse, this uncomfortable buckboard pulled by two ginormous horses moved at a snail's pace. At this rate, he seriously doubted he'd make it down the Cajon Pass before noon.

Nothing had gone according to plan so far. Landing in Hesperia at least fifty miles from Granite Heights. Discovering no horses available to rent. Sleeping in a barn between grunting pigs, cows, and horses. Barely getting any shuteye. Add that to an itchy wool blanket thrown over a couple of bales of hay, most likely filled with bugs, he scratched his head and pulled out a long piece of straw.

Concentrate on something else. He checked out the

rows of oranges planted where the Interstate 15 would be one day.

"We should be there within the hour."

He reached into his pocket for his cell phone to check the time. Right. By now his phone was dead.

"Any idea what time it is now?"

"Ten or eleven." The man adjusted his straw hat. The horses clopped along kicking up dirt with their hoofs.

"I need to be in Granite Heights by two."

Do you have any suggestions how I can do this?" If only he had his truck or even his motorcycle, he could reach his destination in an hour or two even with heavy traffic.

"Since it's Saturday, I wouldn't count on the train. Seems lately something is always blocking the tracks."

"Then I'll head for the livery." Hopefully, he'd find a horse this time.

"Smart man. What's in Granite Heights?"

"My girl."

"Any reason why you have to see her today?"

"To stop a wedding."

"Think she'll be happy to see you?"

"That's what I'm counting on." Passing the San Bernardino Mortuary, the farmer turned up E Street and pointed to a two-story brick building. "That's the Opera House where I got to hear Maude Adams. She sings sweeter than a canary."

"Really?" The concert was probably the highlight of this farmer's life.

"I'm turning here. Whoa." The man slowed his horses to a stop. "Head east about ten blocks, up one street and you'll arrive at the Star Livery.

"Thanks for the ride." Garrett shook the guy's hand.

"You're welcome. Good luck with your gal."

"I'm gonna need it." He needed way more than luck to pull this off.

GARRETT RAN several blocks when he came to Basil's Brewery. After his crazy morning, what he would give to have a beer about now. But he kept on going, past the St. Charles Hotel, and the First National Bank. Four more blocks and up one street, he spotted the livery sign and would've shouted, *Yes,* if he had enough breath to do so.

Instead he had to wait at the corner for a carriage to go by before he crossed the rutted dirt road. Keeping his eyes fixed on the three horses tied near the livery door, of course, he ended up stepping in a pile of road apples in the middle of the street.

He stomped to remove most of the gunk from the bottom of his boots and walked under the covered entry into a livery double the size of the one in Hesperia. Four buggies and two wagons filled the open area. Horses nickered and whinnied from the stalls two deep.

"That's a good boy," an older gentleman pulled out an apple, feeding a chestnut bay. The horse crunched the food in two seconds. "What can I do for you?" The man turned.

"I'd like to rent a horse."

"Can't help you there. I stable or sell them. This one's a hundred dollars."

Garrett kept his expression serious while he fought the gasp he swallowed. A hundred dollars in this era would be worth two or three thousand in his time.

"That's too steep for me." He shrugged.

"Hmm ... I could let Crackerjack go for fifty." The man motioned to a gray mare in the next stall.

Garrett eased the animal's lip back, noting sagging gums, rounded incisors, and the long front teeth that narrowed on the sides. Definitely old and skinny with scars marring the back. Probably abused. It wouldn't surprise him to have the animal drop dead on him, but what other choice did he have? "She's pretty old," he said shrugging.

"I can throw in the tack his owner left behind."

"Make it forty dollars and you've got a deal."

"Sold." The man shook his hand.

"What's the best route to Granite Heights?"

"Follow Stagecoach Road, take the fork to the left and continue south."

"Will do," Garrett mounted his horse and took off, figuring he had less than three hours to get to the church.

CHAPTER 34

The lacy pink canopy on Josie's bed reminded her of her childhood. She used to pretend her very own knight in shining armor would show up outside and rescue her on his white horse and take her away to her happily ever after.

"You're blushing," her friend, Elizabeth, swished into her room wearing a long pink satin dress. "Dreaming about your groom?"

"Of course." *Not,* she added silently. If only her groom were Garrett. One smile from him and her pulse quickened. When he kissed her—my oh my—her body melted.

"Look at you. My best friend is in love." Elizabeth hugged her.

The familiarity of her lavender scent brought back memories of the two of them picking wildflowers on their way to school as kids. She hugged her back, her arms feeling as heavy as her heart had become.

"Are you nervous about your wedding night?"

A cold chill shivered through her. Tolerating William's kisses had been bad enough. Now she would have to sleep with him.

"Don't worry. The first time's not that bad, really. I mean it will hurt for a bit when his manhood joins with you, but after that ... well .... it's kind of fun." Elizabeth fanned her face. "And before you know it, you'll be carrying his child." She patted her rounded belly.

Josie really should break off the engagement. But it wasn't like she'd ever tell him about her indiscretion or that he'd even notice. Dash it all. Sweat beaded on her forehead. Her hands were clammy. Her body limp.

"Josie, are you all right?" Elizabeth asked.

She concentrated on her breathing, slow and steady. "I am fine." She focused on her hands instead of directly at her friend because if she did, Elizabeth would know something was wrong with her.

"Drink this." Elizabeth handed her a glass of water. "Have you eaten anything this morning?"

She'd skipped breakfast in the morning room because she hadn't wanted to run into her father.

She hadn't wanted to see anyone. Slowly sipping the water, she placed her glass on the nightstand.

"Here." Elizabeth took a plate of scones left on the bureau and handed it to her. "Eat."

Josie ate three scones. Once consumed, truth be told, she did feel a smidgen better.

Hilda, the household servant entered. "Ready for me to do your hair." Last night after Josie washed her tresses, Hilda had tied the strands up in rags.

"How does a chignon with curled tendrils sound?"

"Lovely." Josie moved to the vanity and gazed into the mirror seeing that the heart and soul of her existence would forever remain in another century.

But she had to go on with the wedding. She could do without luxuries. She didn't need fancy clothes, a fancy house, or prestige. But she did need to eat. William would provide for her. If she were lucky, his business would keep him so busy he wouldn't have much time to focus on her.

An hour later, Josie stood in front of her floor-length mirror. Tiny rose beadwork adorned her satin dress. A high collar buttoned down with pearls.

Her sleeves were made of lace matching the inlays in her skirt.

Her mother wore this fairytale gown. Had she dreamed of happily ever after when she married Josie's father?

"You make such a beautiful bride." Elizabeth dabbed a white handkerchief to her eyes. "I told myself I wouldn't cry. Remember how we used to talk about each of us marrying our perfect Prince Charming?

"I do."

"And now that wish is about to come true for you as it has for me."

If only she could marry the man of her dreams, but she would be fine. Really, she would.

"You look gorgeous." Elizabeth adjusted her veil. "I wish your mom could be here to see you. Remember how we used to help her in the garden. I loved picking her yellow and red zinnias and bringing home a basket of flowers. I see you added them to your bouquet."

"Adding them makes me feel like she's here in spirit." She missed her mom every day. If only she were here now. What would she think about her decision to enter into a loveless marriage? Tears filled her eyes, and she pressed a hand against her chest, refusing to give in to the grief keening through her soul.

Elizabeth took her hand and squeezed it. "I'm sure she's looking down on you and smiling."

Would she be? Josie had her doubts.

"The carriage is downstairs," Claymore called from the doorway.

Josie plastered on a grin. Time for the charade.

CHAPTER 35

Josie waited in the doorway of the church. Colorful lights danced off the stain glass window—the green reminding her of Garrett's eyes. Her throat tightened and pain gripped her heart. She'd never see him again.

Waiting at the back of the church, she clutched her father's arm for some stability. Something to keep her grounded behind the sea of people who filled the pews.

Josie fiddled with the lace on her high neck collar.

"You look just like your mother." Her father's eyes were misty with affection. "Every time I look at you, I see her." He kissed her forehead. "You have her smile, her eyes, her spirit."

The pathetic part of her knew she craved his attention.

The organist played the Wedding March.

He beamed at her with a father's satisfaction that he made the right match for his daughter. "Let's get you married."

The air deflated in her lungs. "Father, I can't marry William."

"Shh," he whispered in her ear. "We've already settled this."

With each step down the aisle, her heart thumped akin to a stick hitting a drum in a funeral procession. She clutched her father's arm and glanced at the man standing at the front, wearing a dark suit.

They reached the altar, and her father passed her off to William. "He's a good man," he said softly. "Be happy."

William squeezed her hands with his soft non-calloused ones. His touch did nothing to her. She eyed the groom's pinstriped suit, expensive, tailor-made, flattering his tall frame. Her eyes drifted to his square jaw. William was a handsome man, distinguished with flecks of silver in his hair.

"You're beautiful," he said in a low tone.

Hells bells. She couldn't breathe.

"Dearly beloved," the preacher said.

Josie wanted to run down the aisle, out the door

and back to the future. William deserved a wife who loved him.

"We are gathered here to join this man and woman in holy matrimony." She glanced at her father, his smile beaming. Elizabeth's mother pressed a handkerchief against her eyes, and as Josie looked around, so did as half the town.

"William Michael Forsythe, do you take Josephine Anne Goodwin to be your lawfully wedded wife, to love and to cherish from this day forward, in sickness and in health till death do you part?"

"I do," William said.

"Do you, Josephine Anne Goodwin, take William Michael Forsythe to be your lawfully wedded husband …"

Her hands felt clammy.

"To love and to cherish from this day forward …"

Her pulse flittered through her veins.

"In sickness and in health till death do you part."

Her mouth became parched and she swallowed hard. A dull ring filled her ears as the preacher turned to her. She tilted her head and her eyes pleaded with her father. *Please forgive me.* Sweat dripped from her forehead and into her eyes. Tiny black dots danced in front of her. Her eyes rolled up to the ceiling for a sign she was making the right decision.

The preacher cleared his throat waiting for her to consent to her vows.

"I … I … can't marry you."

She dropped her flowers. Heard gasps. Murmurs buzzing around her. Still, she took one step, then another and another. Ten more steps and she'd reach the door of the church.

CHAPTER 36

"Faster," Garrett shouted at the slow nag and kicked his heels into its side, but the horse just trotted along like it had all the time in the world when every second counted. "Come on you damn horse."

The old bag of bones just snorted and continued on with its slow, jarring trot.

The fingers in his left hand were numb. His shoulder twinged. Every bone in his body ached from too many hours in the saddle.

How many times had he heard his father lecture? *Real men don't give up when things get tough.*

You're absolutely right, he silently thought.

Then he checked out his path. Great! He must've taken the wrong fork because he moved away from the railroad tracks. So he turned back the way he came down the path and headed up the correct fork.

The wind whirled around him whispering, *'You'll never measure up. You're just not good enough.'*

Stop.

'Real men don't give up.' His father's words echoed through his head.

"Josie needs me," he called back. "I can't fail her."

A wooden signpost appeared around the next bend.

Granite Heights—2 miles.

"We're almost there," he told Crackerjack hoping the mare would pick up her tempo. Of course she didn't. Passing the cemetery, he let out a sigh.

A bell from the distant tower clanged two times.

He reached into the front pocket of his vest and unfolded the paper. Okay, that street on the corner must be it. A wagon drove past him kicking up dirt, forcing him to blink several times and with watery eyes he memorized the note.

He headed east down Main Street, kneeing the horse to a trot. People milled along the boardwalk. Men smoked cigars in front of the general store. A line formed outside the bakery. He reached the schoolhouse and turned right. One more block. Chapel Street. He spotted the town hall and then the church.

"Yes." He fisted the air. He made it.

Now to stop the wedding.

He dropped the reins and slid from the horse.

Pulling on the door, it squeaked. Heads turned back staring at him, mouths agape.

"G-Garrett?" Josie spoke in a faint whisper, stopping a few feet in front of him close to the door.

He gazed at Josie, beautiful with her red hair swept up in a chignon while her gown accented her curves.

Dammit. He must be too late. His stomach twisted.

"Don't marry that guy." He took a step closer watching her confused eyes flicker to his. "Josie?'

She stood there and stared at him like he was a ghost.

"I love you."

"You l-love me."

Did her stutter mean she was upset? What if she didn't love him? Well, he'd managed to cross through time to get to her. And he couldn't stop talking now. Pleading. "Of course I'm in love with you. I think I fell for you the moment we met." He reached for her hand. "I'd like you to come back with me."

"Who the hell is he?" a deep voice grumbled.

He looked around the church and saw a room full of eyes gaping at him. His focus drifted to the alter. The frown on the groom's face alarmed Garrett. The last thing he wanted was more trouble.

"His name is Garrett Kellogg." Josie interrupter, as she clutched Garrett's hand as she turned toward a graying man at the front pew. Garrett assumed the guy was her father.

"What's wrong with you, Josie? You belong with William."

"No, I don't. I never should have gone ahead with the ceremony. William, I c-can't marry you."

"You are not picking this cowboy over me?" William's face reddened as he shouted the words.

"I am." Josie lifted her chin. God, he loved her spirit.

"It's your loss," William huffed, turned on his heels, and stomped out the side door.

Murmurs sounded around Garrett, but he didn't pay them any mind. Right now, all he cared about was Josie. As her father approached them, she squeezed his hand like he were her very own life support.

"I think you're making a mistake." Her father's brows rose.

"Your wrong father. Garrett is the good man." Her hands trembled. "The best man I've ever known."

"Hmm …" Her father squinted at Garrett. His lips pinched. "Do you love him?"

"Yes, father."

Her dad looked to Garrett then to his daughter. "Take care of her." A fragile flame of hope moved inside Garrett watching the flicker of understanding flash in her dad's eyes.

"Thank you, Father." She kissed his cheek.

"Josie, we need to catch the train," Garrett said. *"If we don't, we'll miss our portal home,"* he whispered in her ear.

"I must leave." Her eyes filled with tears. "Bye Father."

His stomach tightened. She was giving up her old life to be with him. For him.

She took Garrett's arm, hesitated in the doorway and waved at her dad. "We'll take the carriage."

"Works for me." Garrett seized her hand and they dashed down the steps.

"Head for the horse in buggy out front. It's rented for the rest of the day."

They ran past horses tied out front at the hitching posts, his dapple-gray chomping on the grass and stopped in front of a fancy black carriage pulled by white horses.

"Are you leaving, miss?" the chauffer asked.

"Please take us to the train depot right away," Josie said breathless.

"Yes, miss." The man held the door open for her.

She climbed in first and Garrett sat on the bench next to her.

"Please hurry," she said to the driver and he shut the door.

And they took off. They reached a cross street. "Take a right here. It's a shortcut," she called out the window.

The carriage made a sharp turn. He fell into her, grabbing onto her arms, leaning down he brushed his lips against hers and kissed her. Deep. Passionate. Pouring his heart and soul as their tongues danced. Proving with this simple kiss how much she meant to him. When they pulled apart, he sucked in a deep breath and glanced out the window. The depot came into sight.

The coach stopped. A train sat on the tracks as he got out of the vehicle. The locomotive started moving.

"Hurry." He grabbed her hand. They ran along the platform, lungs starved for oxygen as they made it to an open cattle car.

"Hang onto my hand. We're gonna jump on three," Garrett called. "One. Two. Three." They leaped into the car and both of them fell into the hay.

"We made it." His heartrate thudded hard and fast as he leaned back on his elbows.

"We sure did. I still can't believe you came after me." She pressed her lips against his cheek.

"I'd rather be here with you than anywhere else." He tugged her close, delighting that he held her in his arms. "I'm still surprised it worked. Not that I'm complaining.

"How did you figure out how to find to me?"

"I called Uncle Al. You remember him from the barbecue, right? He's Mickie's husband."

"Of course. He seemed nice."

"Well, he's into black holes and weird astrophysics stuff. Anyway, it turns out my cousin Mia's a time traveler along with your brother."

She squinted her eyes at him. "Wait. Do you mean Dusty's in the future?"

"He sure is. I met him last week, well … sort of last week."

She wrapped her arms around his neck, hugging him tightly. "I can't believe my brother's there. How does he look? Is he okay?"

"He's great. Actually, he's engaged to my cousin."

"Unbelievable." She loosened her hold on him.

"You can say that again. Lately, everything's gone a little wacky."

"There's a whole new future for us. Together we can conquer anything." Her mouth met his.

Garrett still couldn't believe he'd found his way back to her. For the first time ever. he felt like Superman rescuing Lois Lane or Spider-Man saving Mary Jane Watson. The fact that he knew those names said he'd spent far too much time watching romantic movies with his sister. The same sister who refused to fall in love.

He'd thought the same way until he met Josie. She acted like he was good enough. "If everything goes to plan my uncle seems to think the portal will open in Whiskeyville like it did for you when you first arrived. If you hadn't written those letters and left them in that chest, I wouldn't be here."

"I had to try something."

"And we're together." He held her tight not about to ever let her go.

CHAPTER 37

Garrett still couldn't believe he had Josie in his arms—in a wedding dress no less. She'd come so close to marrying someone else out of necessity. A section of her veil covered her face and he flipped it back behind her shoulders and ran his fingers over the smooth skin along her chin.

His eyes collided with her turquoise blue pools which darkened as she smiled at him. His hunger for her grew. He yanked her onto his lap. She fit perfectly like she had always belonged right there with him. Her long dress spilled over his legs and across the hay strewn floor. "You're so beautiful," he said, his voice hoarse. Never in his life had a woman's nearness brought out both passion and a need to be tender and caring. "I've missed you."

"As have I you." She plucked a piece of hay from

his hair, so close her intoxicating flowery scent teased him. Her arms twined around his neck, and heat ricocheted through his body.

He cupped the side of her face in one palm and ran a thumb along her cheek. Those perfect crimson-colored lips stirred something primal inside him as he brought his mouth down over hers. A jolt of energy rooted him to the bone as if he were floating on a cloud. He stayed like that frozen as if time stood still. The two of them together enjoying the moment and staring into each other's eyes.

Massaging her shoulders in slow strokes, she arched toward him. He groaned under his breath and brushed his lips back and forth over her lips. Their mouths fully emerged with a hot deep slide of his tongue. She tasted like honey and mint and everything sweet. Their kisses got hotter, more intense until he panted, starved for her, relishing every second.

Heat burned into his stomach which he attributed to the passion burning between them. They were on fire, or at least he felt that way, until she sharply pulled away from him.

"There's something burning against my bottom."

It took a second to comprehend her words. "I think it's the ruby on my belt buckle. Let's rub the garnet together." Heat shot through his jeans and the material of his boxers. With one hand, he used his fingertips along the quarter-sized stone while her fingertips did the same. He kept his right arm around her waist, holding her.

"Something is happening!" her voice shrieked.

"The compartment vibrated, shook, shimmered with radiant bright lights. The car spun. Colors swirled making it impossible to keep his eyes open.

"This is fantastical." She held an arm around his neck.

"You're telling me?" Chilly air from a vent blew across his neck and cheeks. "And we're together."

"Next stop, Whiskeyville," came from the speaker instead of a porter.

He opened his eyes and sighed. "We made it home."

Josie clutched Garrett's arm as the train stopped. They stepped out of the car in modern day Whiskeyville. At first glance the town could pass for the nineteenth century with the old town buildings and cobblestone streets.

"Except people in your time never wore shorts, T-shirts and flip-flops."

"This is so surreal. The last time I came to this town, you arrested me."

"Turned out to be the smartest thing I've ever done," he crooned.

Were his feet floating as she strolled along the platform because it sure seemed that way? His mouth hurt from smiling so hard. But he couldn't help himself.

"Hey," someone called from right past the depot. "Over here."

"Zack." Garrett kept their hands entwined as he rushed to his friend. "You're a sorry sight to see. How'd you know we'd be here today?"

"Al had a hunch you'd make it back this afternoon. He and Mickie are waiting at the train tracks by the Silver Spur. Kristy headed off to Daggett. We wanted to make sure all the bases were covered." Zack enveloped Josie in a big bear hug. "I'm so glad to see you're back.

"I'm home," she whispered.

"Yes, you are." And Garrett couldn't help grinning from ear to ear.

An hour later after showering and changing at the bunkhouse, Garrett held Josie's hand as they walked into the farmhouse. A fluttery thrill filled her soul knowing she'd finally see her brother again.

"Hello, little bit," Dusty drawled in that sweet tone.

She ran into his arms, reveling in the familiarity of his hay and leather scent. "Oh, Dusty. I've missed you so much." Her eyes filled with tears that dripped down her cheeks. "I can't believe we're together here."

"It's been quite a wild ride." Dusty let go of his hold on her. "I want to introduce you to my fiancé, Mia."

"I've heard all about you," a pretty woman with stunning green eyes beamed adoringly at her brother.

Dusty's grin shown with mischief.

She let out a big release of breath. Her dear brother. Still tall and handsome, his eyes crinkled at the corners.

"I can't thank you enough for rescuing Josie." Dusty shook Garrett's hand.

"You should've seen him. He was wonderful." Josie kissed Garrett's cheek and moved to the couch with him sitting next to her. "He crashed into the church just as I'd walked away from my groom and rescued me."

"It didn't go as easy as I'd hoped. We got to the depot just as the train took off and had to sprint to catch it and managed to jump into a cattle car."

"But we made it, and I get to see my favorite brother."

Dusty chuckled. "I'm your only brother."

"Still, my favorite." She giggled feeling lighter, like a younger version of herself.

"Good to hear. I wish you would have told me about how unhappy you were with your father." Dusty held Mia's hand.

"I was fine really." She almost sluffed off the truth, putting on the mask she'd mastered over the years, but she wasn't that person anymore. She didn't need to fabricate an answer that would appease her father. "I mean, life with father could never measure up to my summers spent at the Silver Spur, but I had friends. I got to ride Duchess and paint in the garden. And I would have been content staying in Granite Heights if father had not decided I needed a husband. He actually picked one of his business partners as my intended."

"That's plain wrong." Dusty fisted his hands.

"In fairness, I believe he thought he was doing what was best for me. Father has this black and white view of right and wrong. He didn't want me to end up a spinster." She couldn't help defending him, but he was her father after all. "Anyway, that part of my past is done. Let's celebrate the fact I'm here now."

"Why don't we sit?" Al motioned to the living room. "Who wants beer?'

Garrett put his hand to her back as he led her to one of the chairs and pulled her onto his lap. The minute her eyes collided with Garrett's a zing of awareness warmed her from inside out. She loved this man.

The afternoon went on. They ate submarine sandwiches and reminisced about old times with friends and family. She learned that Mia was an artist like her, but she specialized in graphic design. They even set up a meeting where Mia planned to introduce Josie to an integrated computer program called Adobe.

Josie couldn't help smiling. In the same location where she spent so many happy summers, she found herself surrounded by people she loved—exactly where she belonged.

CHAPTER 38

Later that evening, Zack and Kristy had headed off to work. Garrett and Josie had the house to themselves.

Josie wore a short sundress and eased into the couch next to him. "Is something the matter?"

"Nothing at all. I'm just glad we're together." Garrett set his arm around her shoulders. "Are you tired?"

"I should be but I'm not. I think I'm still high on this unbelievable day."

"It has been insane." He gazed into her pretty turquoise eyes, eyes he thought he might never see again. "I really liked your letters."

"You mean when I said I'd given up. I felt like such a failure."

"You're the strongest, smartest, most resilient

woman I've ever met. When you said you loved me, I knew I do anything to get to you."

"Oh, Garrett, that's so romantic."

"That's me. Mr. Romance," he chuckled. "You know, I think I fell for you the moment I slapped handcuffs onto your dainty wrists. It was your pretty blue eyes. They get me every time."

She fluttered her lashes. What a tease.

"Obviously, you were upset when I arrested you, but all the while you managed to hold it together … that is until I mentioned your dad."

"It's been ingrained in me that women are to suppress undue emotions and never cause a fuss. Although I never truly mastered that skill. I spent many an hour confined to my room for such outbursts." She lowered her head.

"I bet you hated that." He tried to picture her as a determined little girl probably a bit precocious.

"It wasn't that bad. I had at least a dozen dolls to confide in." She gave a soft chuckle. "Plus, my mom usually would come in and join me. I don't recall ever hearing her argue with my dad, but she had her own way of getting around him. Still, I often wondered if they were happy together. Her eyes never lit up like they did when she talked about Dusty's dad."

"How 'bout you? Do your eyes light up when you talk about me?"

"I have no idea, but my lips sizzle when you kiss me." She ran her finger along the top one.

"Do they now? Let's see if it's the same for me?" Running his thumb underneath her jawline, he tipped her chin and moved in to tease her pliant lips. "Have I told you how stunning you look in that dress?"

"No." She leaned over and brought her sweet soft, searing hot mouth against his cheek.

He stared at her for a long moment. Taking in her heart-shaped face, the slight tilt of her chin, her sultry gaze. This gorgeous lady with such a zest for life had ensnared his mouth, ensnared his soul, ensnared his very essence, and he didn't mind. Not one little bit. "You're perfect."

"So are you." She grasped the collar of his T-shirt and snagged him closer.

He ran his hand along her shoulder, bare except for the spaghetti straps of her dress. Whispering kisses along the nape of her neck, he gave a little nip at her collarbone, sniffing in her clean, floral scent.

She snaked her arms around his neck, pulling him down to her. Their lips touched. An instant yearning shot through every one of his nerve endings. Intoxicating. Fascinating. Delicious. One kiss, one simple kiss and he swam in a heated red zone.

He pulled down the top of her dress and gazed at her lacy bra. When he cupped a breast with his hand over the thin fabric, she let out a little moan. His mouth watered. He wanted to taste every part of her. "I want you in my bed, Josie." He put his thumb under her chin and forced her to face him.

"Yes."

He paused for a second and turned away. "I'd like to carry you but don't think my shoulder can handle it."

"I can walk."

"I know you can, but it's hard for me. I hate admitting I'm broken." He tangled his fingers through her silky hair floating down her shoulders in a soft cascade of waves.

"Come on, Garrett. Do you think I care if you have an injured shoulder or hand for that matter? I love you just the way you are." She kissed him for the longest time. "I thought we were heading for your bedroom?"

"Miss Goodwin, are you trying to seduce me?"

"Absolutely." She grabbed his hand, tugging him, and they ran up the stairs.

Turned on beyond belief, he kicked the door open to his room with a thud, and he pulled her dress over her head. His cock jumped as he stared at her bare body except for the scraps of lace covering her breasts and the thong patch covering her womanly parts. "You're so pretty."

She reached for his shirt and tugged it over his head. Then her fingers roamed along his abs. One hand reached for his belt buckle. She unzipped his pants and they dropped to the floor. "Now, we're even." She brought her mouth to one of his nipples and licked it.

"Holy shit."

"You like that, huh?" she asked.

"Damn straight." He pushed her back on the bed and moved to her side, feathering kisses along her jawline while capturing her rosy pink bud with his tongue and making it pucker to a hard rock. "How's that?"

"Mmm," she purred, while hot fingertips explored his chest, his abs, his back.

He brought his mouth to hers, grazing on those warm, petal soft lips against his and kissed her for the longest time. "I'll never tire of this."

"Me neither," she sighed. "Don't ever let me go."

"I won't." He wanted her right where she was.

He concentrated on the other nipple, and she rewarded him with a soft hum. He got a full view of her slim waist, her stomach, her navel. He loved that navel and tracked down to it with his tongue twirling around the center. He gazed down to her legs and the juncture between them covered up with a skimpy patch of underwear.

Slow down. You've got all night.

He retreated away from her stomach and brought his lips back to her mouth, kissing her, deeply. She joined in seeming just as eager as he. His hand drifted down beneath that scrap of material and ran a thumb over her clit while his finger dipped inside her warm, wet opening.

She squirmed. "I want more."

He stoked her pussy, finding her tight and wet and enchanting. Her tiny nub slick with desire. A temptress driving him wild with those little whimpers.

He had to taste her. Removing her panties, he groaned when he saw her red thatch of curls. Positioning his head between her thighs, his tongue swirled over her clit. It didn't take long before she cried out his name. Her body undulated and quavered as she rode her orgasm.

When she finally stopped quaking, he moved away and pulled a square wrapper from his wallet and stared at her for a moment.

"You're not playing fair. Take off those skivvies."

"Skivvies?" he chuckled. "They're called boxers."

He pulled down the garment, her darkened eyes watching him.

"Please, Garrett, make love to me." Her lips skimmed against his jaw.

Taunt with need, he unwrapped the condom, rolled it on, spread her legs, nudging them apart.

His breath crawled sluggishly through his lungs as he positioned himself against her entrance. He tilted his hips, claiming her inch by inch until he filled her completely. Bringing his mouth to hers, he kissed her gently allowing her a moment for her body to relax as he pulled out. He slowly pushed back inside her. She arched against him, urging him on. He could no longer think. Could only feel. His focus attuned to merging the two of them into one. They were lost in sensation as they deepened the exchange. A slow burn before the inferno coming together forming one entity.

She wrapped her legs around his waist. Her core clenching him as she shattered. Her tremors washing against him. "Oh, Garrett!" Her frenzied cry brought him over the edge.

He shoved inside her one last time, shuddering as he exploded, wave after wave skyrocketing to bliss. His overheated body splintering to a million pieces. Only Josie could drive him to pleasure town like this.

He collapsed on top of her, too spent to move. When his breathing slowed and his heart stopped thudding against his chest, he brought her to his side and wrapped his arms around her. "Holy shit. That was good. No wonder I love you."

EPILOGUE

The last nine months went by like a blur. Living at the bunkhouse and sharing her life with Garrett had been good, really good. Every night after he got off work, she greeted him in his bed. Their bed now.

But they needed their own space. When Garrett suggested they fix up the old foreman cabin on the Silver Spur property, she was all in, helping him take down walls, adding a bathroom, running water, electricity. Next weekend, they planned to move in.

Living together was commonplace for this century. And they'd done so for months in the bunkhouse. But for some odd reason this house seemed like a massive step for both of them. Maybe because they'd worked as a team, maybe because it would be theirs, maybe because it permanently sealed their love cementing her heart and soul to him.

But today she focused on the Founder's Day Celebration. Even though Garrett wasn't the sheriff this year, he insisted they wear the same outfits as last year. Mia and Dusty were joining them. Newlyweds. She was happy for her brother.

Josie had found her home in this wondrous new land with a perfect man.

His lips quirked up as he pulled into the Whiskeyville parking lot. She stared at his profile, his square jaw shaved clean and that wide mouth that could drive her crazy. He opened her car door and held her hand as they walked past the blacksmith shop with an anvil clanging, and by the old livery where a man hooked up a horse and carriage. Garrett stopped at the door of the jailhouse.

"You gonna arrest me again, sheriff?" She clutched his arm.

"Maybe later, babe. I left my handcuffs at home."

"Promises, promises." Her face flamed. Last week he'd handcuffed her to the bedpost and made love to her.

His lips quirked up. Garrett proved to be quite an inventive lover. He put his arm around her and led her by the toy shop and the visitor's center.

"Are we going to the Shooting Gallery Grill?"

"Yep."

"Back to where we shared our first meal together. How romantic." The event seemed like forever ago.

He squeezed her hand. "Except this time we won't be alone."

Dusty stood and waved his hat. "Over here."

They weaved their way between some families near the walkway and back to a long table in the middle not far from the front of the burger place and took a seat facing the boardwalk.

"Mickie and Al are in line. You text him your order yet?" Mia asked.

"Did that last night." Garrett had a glint in his eye that she couldn't quite read. Something was definitely up with him.

"Hope we're not late." Zack and Kristy rushed in and sat across from her and Garrett.

"My fault. Bad hair day. Thank goodness I had this." Kristy tugged on her wide-brimmed straw hat. The pink color matched her sundress.

"I think it's cute." Josie laughed. Kristy had taught her to embrace fashion and so much more since they'd become friends.

Al edged his way toward them carrying two cup holders with four drinks in each. "Sarsaparilla for you, Josie," he set the drink in front of her first and passed out other sodas to the group before sinking into one of the empty seats.

Mickie handed out burgers and fries and took the last spot. “Let’s toast being together.” She held up her cup and everyone tapped their drinks.

Garrett wore a goofy smirk as he put his arm on the back of her chair.

“How was Hawaii?” Kristy asked.

“Fabulous. I talked Dusty into snorkeling.” Mia giggled.

“Didn’t think I’d like being trapped in one of those face masks but found it worth trying. Never knew ocean fish could be so colorful.” Dusty’s beaming smile said he’d had fun. “Plus, I got to spend a week with Mia in a bikini.” He nuzzled her neck.

“Okay, you guys,” Zack said. “TMI.”

“So, what’s up for the rest of the day,” Josie asked.

“Stuff.” Garrett chuckled. “If everyone’s done, let’s go.”

Talk about being evasive. “Dash it all. Why are you smirking?”

“You’ll see soon enough,” he chuckled.

“No fair.” She dropped his hand. He secured his arm around her shoulders and tugged her closer.

The streets were filled with an assortment of people from young to old. The clock tower chimed three times as they passed the cigar shop. Men gathered around some guy whittling. Probably the same guy she'd seen last year.

She glanced across the street. "We haven't been here since we arrived from the 1890s."

"Come on." He held her hand as they walked across the street with Mia, Dusty, Al, Mickie, Kristy and Zack. A locomotive started up on the closest track heading south. Steam chuffed from a pipe on the side.

A flash of fear tinged up her spine. No way did she want to go back in time. Reaching for her locket, she remembered tucking her necklace in the farmhouse attic along with Dusty's belt buckle and Mia's ring. No need to worry about opening a portal. Thank goodness. She let out a long sigh.

"You okay?" Garrett stopped right in front of the engine.

"Dandy … well … for a second I worried about going back."

"You're not going anywhere without me next to you." He rocked on the heels of his cowboy boots. His hands clenched at his sides. His expression stone serious.

"What's wrong?" She grasped the strap of her purse so tightly her hand hurt. Why was he acting odd?

"Nothing at all. Josie, you are the best thing to

ever come into my life. You've taught me to trust in myself. Every day with you keeps on getting better and better. I love you, Josie Goodwin." He pulled out a black box from his pocket, got down on one knee and pointed to the banner hanging several yards past the Founder's Day sign, his eyes shining.

Josie, will you marry me?

"You did all this for me?" He'd proclaimed his love for her to the world. The sheer magnitude of his actions made her giddy. Happiness burst inside of her like a shooting star granting her deepest wish.

"What do you say, Josie? Will you be my wife?" His eyes rounded with concern.

Did he really think she might refuse him? "Y-yes, Garrett," she said. It felt as if she were floating off the ground. This gorgeous man loved her. He wanted her forever.

He slipped a ring on her finger. Not a diamond. Not a garnet, but a blue topaz that sparkled in the sunlight. Her favorite stone. He swung her around a few times. People clapped including her friends.

Cocooned in his embrace, she basked in the delicious combination of happiness and absolute contentment.

His mouth descended on hers and he kissed her for the first time as her fiancé. The slow restraint filling her as their hearts and minds melded and their breathing intermingled. He showed her how much he truly cared, worshipping her with an all-consuming heat. "You're the best thing to ever happen to me."

"As are you." She sighed, gazing up at her tall drink of masculinity. "I'll love you forever."

All her life she had dreamed of a love like this. Sighing contently, she snuggled closer to him knowing she was truly home.

With Garrett she found her happily ever after.

The End

If you enjoyed TIME FOR LOVE, you might want to read TIME TO SAVE A COWBOY from my Western Romance Time Travel Series.

The Cowboy Doesn't Deserve to HANG

Captivated by the story of a cowboy hanged as a horse thief in 1890, Mia Kellogg travels back in time with only thirty days to save an innocent man.

Dusty Mann is determined to buy his own ranch.

He doesn't need a modern, straightforward woman to barrel into his life or knock his plans off track.

But Mia steals his heart—and then says she's from the future.

Read an excerpt from TIME TO SAVE A COWBOY

In front of Mia, a gentleman in a dark suit and top hat assisted a lady into her carriage seat. The driver positioned himself to her left and picked up the reins. His horse neighed.

Mia shifted back a few steps, giving the horse plenty of room as she leaned her elbows against a railing behind her. The buggy took off leaving thin ruts in the powdery dirt.

Hot air raced down her neck. Something hit the back of her head, jerking her forward, pushing her, making her stumble into the street. She gained her footing. Spun around. Her arms pinwheeled. "Stop tha—"

Her words clogged her throat, cut off her breath.

A horse, oh no, a horse.

She stared at its large, triangular brown head inches from her face. No, not large. Gigantic. Her heart tripped in her chest; her legs became immovable.

Its nostrils flared, its obsidian-colored eyes widened.

She tried to move, but her limbs became rigid, her feet cemented in place. The horse stomped one hoof against the ground and swished its tail against its flank. A thousand pounds of imposing beast sniffed the air.

She stood frozen, watching its nostrils flair and flatten, flare and flatten. "Get, get back."

The horse's mouth opened, and it bared teeth the size of playing cards.

Move, she told herself. Move, before it stomps on you.

The horse let out a high-pitched snort and threw its head up.

She was gone, racing down the street, sprinting up the hotel's wide wooden staircase, straight through an open door, running fast. Fear propelled her like a slingshot.

She charged inside and plowed into a solid object with an umph.

"Slow down." Large hands steadied her and released its hold. The man stepped away.

At only five-foot-two, she stared straight at his massive shoulders. This guy must spend hours at the gym. Okay, she had to quit gawking at his chest. She gazed up as he took off his worn-leather Stetson.

He gave her a lopsided grin. "Somethin' troubling you?"

"No." Not wanting to seem like an idiot, she stoned her expression, while her knees wobbled.

"You're kinda pale. Best you sit a spell." He placed his hands on her shoulders and guided her to an overstuffed couch near a brick fireplace. Heat sizzled through her gown's fabric, and her insides tingled.

"Excuse me." The cowboy flagged a waitress in a long black dress and white apron. "I'd be obliged if you brought this lady some water." He relaxed in an adjacent armchair and flashed her a brazen smile. "Never had a beautiful gal barrel into me. What's the hurry, miss?"

"Um, you see, this horse, it scared me. The horse, um, was huge, enormous." Sounding stupid, she concentrated on a multicolored glass-blown vase on the side table and rearranged the orange poppies to be in front of the violets and lupines.

"Must've been one of Ben's Belgian draft horses," he said, and she noticed his russet brown hair touched the top of his shirt collar.

The server handed her a glass of water. She took a sip. "It's warm."

"No surprise. This is the desert." The cowboy's drawl didn't seem practiced.

"I'm not as freaked as—" She looked at him, really looked at him, and recognized those wide-set gray eyes from somewhere. "You look familiar."

"I'd remember meeting a pretty gal like you." His smile lit up his handsome face, and her heart fluttered.

She focused on the people at the front desk. A

clerk slid a key to a man, and he left with a lady in a long chiffon dress. Most likely people from the train.

A heavy-set woman approached her. "I'm Jenny Hayes. My husband, Bob, and I manage the hotel."

"Mia Kellogg." She held out her hand.

Jenny gave her a sideways glance.

Why wouldn't she shake her hand? Must be a germaphobe.

"Saw Dusty walk you in. Did the heat get to you?"

"Maybe a little. I'm fine now." Mia examined his features. His tan complexion set off his wolf gray eyes. He was a ringer to the cowboy from the picture in the antique shop. "Your name's Dusty?"

He straightened and rewarded her with a mischievous grin. "Yep."

"His given name's Harold Mann, but folks have been calling him Dusty since he was knee high to a grasshopper." Jenny butted in. She must be related to him somehow. "What brings you to our town?"

"A short vacation."

"Well, you certainly chose an ideal time for your stay. Tomorrow's our monthly ball." Jenny's cheeks reddened.

Now Mia was confused. She and Birdie had tickets for the Daggett dance. Maybe she got the name of the town wrong. Still, if her relatives were here, she should have seen them by now. "Could I borrow your phone and call my cousin?" Mia asked, anxious to talk with someone she knew.

"Golly, we don't have a telephone here. Our general store is the only business in town that has one. The shop's closed 'till morning," Jenny said.

Mia's throat got tight. Only one phone in town. This took the turn-of-the-last-century thing a bit far.

"I imagine you're famished, miss. May I find you a table in the dining room?"

"Please." Starved, at least her stomach didn't rumble.

Jenny turned to Dusty. "Will you be joining Miss Kellogg?"

Mia expected him to refuse politely. Not say, "I'd be honored." He stood and offered his arm. His scent of leather and masculinity made her lean closer. Wrong response for a guy she'd just met.

Jenny led the two of them through the spacious ballroom. Mia's right foot hit a slick, polished spot on the hardwood flooring. "Oh no."

Dusty tightened his grasp on her arm. "Careful, darlin'."

Was her lightheadedness from lack of food or … was it him? She took small mindful steps to their linen covered table. Mindful of the waxed floor. Mindful of clutching his muscular biceps.

"Here you go." He pulled out her chair. His gray eyes darkened when he looked at her. He appeared well-mannered, but she wondered if his kisses would hold a bad boy edge. She couldn't believe she thought about kissing him. Not exactly appropriate for a guy she barely knew—but he was cute.

Her eyes drifted to the five-o'clock shadow on his chin. Certain she'd been caught staring, she unfolded her napkin and placed it on her lap.

"Enjoy your meal," Jenny said and scurried off.

Mia should be looking for her phone, but hunger won out. She knifed jelly on a roll and bit into the warm orange-flavored dough. Wickedly scrumptious. She drank from a crystal glass. "The lemonade's sour." A pound of sugar wouldn't take away the tartness.

He held up a crystal bowl. "Want some sugar?"

"Please." She should use Sweet'N Low but being on vacation why not splurge a little? She added three generous teaspoons, deciding she'd make up for her indulgences at spin class on Monday. "What do you do?"

"Do?" His brow rose, and he looked at her like she asked him to explain the theory of relativity.

"Your job."

"Me? I'm a cowhand." His drawl came out a bit over exaggerated.

Her dad regularly watched old westerns. This guy had a casual Gary Cooper presence. She focused on the jagged scar on his chin. She liked the flaw, showed he wasn't plastic-perfect. "Where's your ranch?"

"It's not mine." He winced for a flash. "I'm the foreman of Los Flores Ranch."

The hot cowboy sitting across from her lived in the next town over. Moving back to her hometown suddenly had a big advantage, namely him. She could see him working on the ranch on the outskirts of Hesperia. Lifting bales of hay would explain his beefy arms.

She'd have to give him her number before she left.

<u>TIME TO SAVE A COWBOY</u>

If you enjoyed TIME FOR LOVE, you might want to read COWBOY'S CUPID from my Love's Magic Series.

A Forbidden Love

When Cupid's arrow accidentally strikes the wrong cowboy, she's supposed to fix her mistake—not fall for the alluring mortal.

Cami Calypso receives her first assignment just in time for the Valentine season. As a newbie Cupid Archer, her life is perfect until her arrow accidentally strikes the wrong man. She has sixty days to secure a job as his housekeeper on a ranch and find the cowboy his soul mate—not keep him for herself.

Rhett Holloway needs a housekeeper and cook.

He doesn't need an adorable blonde to distract him.

He doesn't need her to fix his love life.

But here she is, and he finds her irresistible.

Read an excerpt from COWBOY'S CUPID

Rhett had a strange feeling in his gut during dinner. Cami kept checking her watch. He'd asked what bothered her, but she said everything was fine.

After a long day, he helped her clean up the dinner dishes, and they walked to her apartment. Her stance was rigid, her body tense. She didn't shift toward him as he strode with his arm around her shoulder.

"What's wrong?"

"I need to tell you something." She shrugged but wouldn't look at him.

They'd only known each other close to two months, but his heart was all in. He unlocked the apartment door. Seated at the edge of the couch, Cami put a distance between them and avoided eye contact.

"Go ahead." He stood by the kitchen table and waited for a response.

"We were never meant to be together," she said, still not looking his way.

His chest tightened. She was breaking up with him.

"I've got a secret. When I show you, I hope you'll still love me."

"Whatever you've done in the past doesn't matter. We'll get through it." He'd made his share of mistakes.

She extracted a glass vial from her pocket. It sparkled and shimmered. “It’s not what I’ve done, it’s what I am.”

“What are you?” He didn’t even see a flicker of a smile.

Her lips tightened into a grimace. “Please listen carefully to what I say.”

“All right. Spill.” He tapped the side of his pants.

She licked her lips and took a deep breath. “I told you I was a Cupid when you took me to the archery range.”

“Okay.”

She folded her arms. “I live in Zeus’ Kingdom up in the clouds.”

His teeth ground, as he sat next to her and said sarcastically, “Of course you do.”

“You’ve seen my archery skills. Even said I was talented.” She lifted her chin and blew out a breath. “I am a Cupid, a real live Cupid.”

“That’s crazy.” Maybe she was crazy. His primal instinct told him to leave, but he couldn’t move.

“My occupation is an archer.” Tears pooled in her eyes. “I’m telling you the truth.”

“If you’re leaving me, say so, and quit making up this lame story.”

“I don’t want to go anywhere.” She twirled a curl around her finger.

"You don't? And here I thought you were breaking up with me."

"If only things were different. I've got to return home." She looked at her watch.

"So, you are leaving me? Why?" He was confused.

"I don't want to. I'm happy here." Her body slumped, her chin dropped. "My whole life I've dreamed of being good enough."

"But you are good enough." She was the best thing to ever happen to him. "You're perfect for me."

"Don't make me cry, please let me finish." Her eyes softened. "I've dreamed of visiting Earth and infusing humans with arrows of love. When I got my first earthly assignment, I hit the wrong man, namely you."

Those blue eyes. "You shot me with your arrow of love?"

"It was a mistake. My assignment ducked, and I hit you instead. I was sent to rectify my mishap and set you up with your soulmate. We were never supposed to fall in love."

"You love me." His spirits soared.

"Yes."

"'Bout time you admitted it." He moved closer, but she backed up, out of his reach.

"Will you accept the real me?"

"What do you mean? The real Cami's right in

front of me."

"Watch." Rocking back and forth on her heels, her cheeks flushed to a rosier red.

His eyes riveted to her hands.

She unscrewed the glass vial and poured out a glittery substance. Iridescent pink dust swirled and surrounded her. Her body shrunk to the size of a doll, dressed in a shimmering gown. Iridescent wings formed at her shoulders. She flew up midway between the floor and the ceiling.

"Holy shit!" He stared, not frightened, confused.

"I'm a C-Cupid." Her words came out broken.

He froze, became immobile. "This can't be happening."

"I love you, always will." She hovered close to him, and he felt her lips kiss his cheek.

"It's unreal."

"Tell me about it." Her eyes were wide. Wary.

"You really are a Cupid?"

"Yes. Do you still love me?"

He didn't know what to think. "It's too much." He turned his back to her, put his head in his hands.

His girlfriend—a ruler-sized pixie. It couldn't be true.

Except he'd seen her.

COWBOY'S CUPID

Romance Novels by Niki Mitchell

COWBOY'S CUPID

TIME TO SAVE THE COWBOY

REBEL'S CUPID

TIME FOR LOVE

FIREBRAND'S CUPID

LOVE'S HIGH TIDE

Children's Books by Niki Mitchell

KURIOUS KATZ

KURIOUS KATZ AND THE BIG MOVE

KURIOUS KATZ AND THE PLAY DAY

KURIOUS KATZ AND THE NEW FRIEND

KURIOUS KATZ AND THE BIRTHDAY PARTY

KURIOUS KATZ AND THE HALLOWEEN COSTUMES

KURIOUS KATZ AND THE CHRISTMAS TREE

KURIOUS KATZ AND THE BEST CHRISTMAS EVER

FOSTER CATS: ARTEMIS AND HER SNEAKY BROTHER HERCULUES

KURIOUS KATZ AND THE FOURTH OF JULY

KURIOUS KATZ AND THE VALENTINE SURPRISE

KURIOUS KATZ AND THE SNICKERDOODLE STORY

COMING SOON

PRECIOUS PUPS: BREEZY, THE LABRADOR RETRIEVOR

ABOUT THE AUTHOR

Niki Mitchell writes children's books along with contemporary fantasy and historical time-travel romance. She was born in Chicago, Illinois, and moved to Whittier, California in first grade. With a houseful of books and a local library located a few short blocks, her love of reading began at a young age.

Married for over thirty years and a romantic at heart, she enjoys writing about strong female characters in unusual settings. When she isn't playing with her cats, she enjoys reading, taking walks, water aerobics, photography, and traveling.

Dear Readers,

Thank you for reading TIME FOR LOVE.

I hope you enjoyed my story as much as I enjoyed writing it. Won't you please consider leaving a review? Even just a few works would help others decide if the book is right for them.

Best regards and thank you in advance.

Niki Mitchell

I look forward to forward to hearing from my readers.

Visit me at

https://nikimitchell.weebly.com/

Follow me on FaceBook at

author Niki J. Mitchell

Twitter Niki Mitchell@NikiMitchell7

Instagram

NikiJMitchellAuthor

www.ingramcontent.com/pod-product-compliance
Lightning Source LLC
Chambersburg PA
CBHW030333310726
48979CB00001B/15

9781951581213